Three Are One

Dani Haviland

USA Today Bestselling Author

Three Are One is a work of fiction. Names, place, characters, and incidents are the product of the author's imagination and are used for the readers' enjoyment. Any resemblance to persons living, dead, or fictional, events or business establishments is entirely coincidental.

Book Description

Kizzie's husband shunned their special needs daughter and volunteered for Iraq to avoid his family and engage in nefarious operations that ended in his death. The post chaplain tried to help the young widow adjust, but would his feelings for her and the search for his lost sister cause problems?

Acknowledgment

Thanks to LL for suggesting the name Kizzie. I never would have thought of that one on my own! Readers are the fuel that drive my passion for creating stories. Thanks to all of you!

Thanks to all who serve, too. The bad guy in this story is *totally fictional!* I doubt that he'd still be in the U.S. Army if this was based on a true story.

Chapter 1

JBER Joint Base Fort Richardson Elmendorf, Alaska
January 2012

Butch frowned as he looked at her in the corner, sucking her thumb, rocking back and forth. "It's just a phase. The doctor said she'll get through it soon. She's confused right now. I'm doing my best, but it's just me."

"I'm working overseas so you can get those fat paychecks. With the base housing and the food allotment, you two are sitting pretty."

"No, not pretty. A father is more than a paycheck. No. Strike that. I've never thought of you in terms of money— even before she was born or we were married—and I never will. What I need now, more than ever, is your emotional support. When she's teething, I'd love a break. Even if you rocked her while I got a nap lying down instead of sitting up in the rocker, it would help. Good Lord, just to take a shower alone and wash my hair with two hands instead of one…"

"Why don't you just call Bea?"

"She has four kids of her own. I don't want to burden her."

"But you want me to… Oh, never mind." Butch bit his tongue before he said words he'd never be able to take back.

"Yes, I want you to share the burden. But also the joys and blessings. And one more remark about how I'm the reason she has Down Syndrome just might get you salt in your coffee, buster. Life just happens!"

Butch looked down at Kizzie from his towering six-foot six-inch height, not even trying to mask his disgust with the argument that had been ongoing for the two years since Zoe's birth.

"Zoe's your daughter. Look at those beautiful green eyes. She certainly didn't get them from me. They're just like yours. I've never cheated on you and never will. You had your chance for a paternity test and turned it down. Still, we can do the cheek swabs any time you want."

He shook his head and reached for the door. "I don't have time for this crap. Same whine, different day. And your whines don't improve with age. I'm outta here."

"Where are you going?"

"Back home."

"But you are home."

"No, I'm not. Home is where you feel needed, wanted.

Where you can do something worthwhile..."

"For God and Country but forget the wife and kid? Oh, what was I thinking when I married you? You know, your rugged good looks came at a terrible sacrifice. The only spine you have is the one the army issued you. When your tour is up, you'll be worthless, unable to stand on your own two feet."

"Then it's a good thing I signed up for another eighteen months. See you then," he said, then walked out. He opened the door a crack and added, "Maybe," the door pulled shut with a *whoosh* of finality.

Kizzie looked out the window and watched as he stepped up into his lifted four-wheel-drive truck and sped away from the house, momentarily spinning out of control before straightening out. "That's all you need—another reckless driving citation. They'll bust you so far down you'll be scrubbing latrines 'til there's peace in the world."

Ring! Ring! Ring!

"Hello?"

"I'd like to speak to my son."

"You'll have to call him on his cell. He just left."

"He didn't pick up, that's why I called the house."

"I'm sorry, Mother Wadsworth, but as I said, he's not here."

"Hmph! Maybe if you were a better wife, he'd stick around longer. I hope you didn't make him mad enough to sign up for another tour! You and that daughter of yours are enough to make a sane man crazy!"

"She has a name, and Zoe is his daughter, too."

Click.

"Well, thanks for asking how we've been, Mother Wadsworth," Kizzie said sarcastically into the phone with no one on the other end. "It was nice talking to you, too. Maybe you can drop by and see your granddaughter. She's almost walking now, you know." She looked at the receiver, shook her head in disgust, and added. "Thank God for small blessings. I'll never move from Alaska if she keeps her word to never set foot in this state again. What a bi…"

Wah! Wah!

"Oh, sweetie, is your mouth hurting you again. Those confounded eye teeth sure make life miserable for you. Here, let me get you your nummy."

Kizzie took Zoe out of her walker and held her close, digging through the frozen peas and carrots to retrieve the blue knobby teething binky. "It's only been in here a few minutes, honey." She put the fluid filled pacifier between her own lips and pretended to chomp down on it. "Yummy, yummy. Cold and soft. Come on, sweetheart. Let's go back to the rocking chair. Mommy needs a time out before she starts throwing things."

***

"Oh, thank you, Bea," Kizzie said, holding back the tears. "I'd love to come over for dinner. I haven't eaten right in days."

"Well, I thought I'd leave you two lovebirds alone for a few days before I called."

"Oh, I guess I didn't tell you. Butch re-upped. I don't know when he's actually getting deployed. He took off in a huff a few days ago and I haven't heard from him since. Zoe and I have been in the rocking chair for days now. I'm not sure who's cried the most."

"Good grief, woman! Why didn't you call me? Can you manage to get the both of you in your car and get over here? I don't have anyone to watch my tribe or I'd come get you. I really need to get a bigger vehicle. I can't fit one more car seat into this one."

"I stink and need a bath before I see anyone…"

"Just grab some clean clothes, her diaper bag, and come on over. I'll watch her while you get a shower over here. The roast is in the oven, I just finished two apple pies, and all we're lacking is you and that beautiful little girl of yours."

"Oh, Bea," Kizzie gushed, her tears blocking off any more words.

"Don't say another word. And if you have dirty clothes, throw them in a duffle and bring them along, too. I know how hard it is to get much done when you have a little one teething."

"I really didn't think teething would take this long…"

Bea changed from consoling friend to big mama mode. "Now, not another word. Hang up, grab your gear, and come on over. LuLu is ready for a little girl to play with. She's bored with all her brothers and keeps asking for a baby sister. Maybe this will keep her happy for a year or five."

***

"I don't know if you realize what a blessing you are, Bea," Kizzie said, handing off her dozing daughter. "Of course, she

6

fell fast asleep as soon as we were out of the garage…"

"That seems to happen to all babies. I'll put her in Tommy's crib for now. The monitor's all set up. Why don't you get your bags and what-not from your car, then head upstairs to the guest bath. I got the kids and dinner covered."

Kizzie leaned in and gave Bea a long hug, absorbing as many positive vibes as she could, trying not to linger too long in her friend's arms. "What am I going to do?"

"I told you, take a shower—or a long bath, if you'd like—then come down for dinner."

"No, I mean about Butch…"

"One dilemma at a time, dear. Life is much more manageable with a full stomach and a clean body. You were here for me when I needed you. I'm just returning the favor."

"You're doing more than that, but you're right. Clean hair always makes me feel better. And is there anything more comforting than the smell of pot roast and apple pie?"

The giggles of children playing filled the pause before she could answer. "Yes, that," Bea said, nodding toward the family room where the older children were playing, "is every bit as comforting. Happy, healthy children interacting with each other is even more wonderful than the scent of cinnamon and beefsteak."

"You're right. I'd better get upstairs or I'll start crying," Kizzie said, then headed up the stairs. *Or I'll start crying all over again!*

'Bath or shower?' went through Kizzie's frazzled mind until she spotted the bowl heaped high with homemade bath bombs, their erratic shape and marbled coloring indicating that this was another of Bea's stay-at-home-with-the-kids projects. She picked through a few of them, took two of the smaller torpedo-shaped ones, sniffed them to make sure she wasn't going to come out smelling like a piece of fruit, then added them to the tub and turned on the water, ready for the first bath she'd had in nearly three years. "Bath first, then shampoo and shower. I may not be queen for a day, but I can be queen for twenty minutes or so." She peeled off the clothes she'd been wearing for two days and nights then knelt to swish the bubbling bath bombs through the water, mixing the scent of lavender and roses throughout.

"You'd think that a good husband would be willing to give his wife at least a little break every once in a while—what's so hard with that?" She paused in her musing as she twisted her hair up into a knot on top of her head, rearranging the mass of curls, and stabbed the black-enamel chopstick back into it. "And there's the answer, smack dab in the middle of the question: a *good* husband. Now what am I going to do?"

She double-checked the water temperature, satisfied that it was mama bear hot and not baby bear tepid, then slipped under the bits of floral petals and leaves. "Ah, just right. I'll solve today's problems tomorrow. Or let them solve themselves. This is my time. No hassles allowed."

Knock, knock, knock. "Are you all right or did you fall asleep?" Bea asked.

"Oh, shoot! I did fall asleep. I'm sorry. I'll be right out."

"No, no worries. Go ahead and finish. I still have to set the table. I just wanted to give you a heads up about dinner," Bea said. "Zoe's awake and having a blast, so don't worry about her."

"Oh, thank you so much. I'll be down in a minute or less," Kizzie said, the tub already draining.

"As long as you don't mind reheating your dinner in the microwave, you can stay in there for another hour, if you'd like."

"Oh, no, no, no. I'll be down in a few minutes. I still need to wash my hair."

"Help yourself to whatever you see. I'll tell you all about them when you come down to eat."

"Thanks," Kizzie said, then got ready for her shower. It was then she noticed. There was not one bottle of commercial shampoo, conditioner, or body soap in the shower. She opened the container with the hand-drawn label 'lilac shampoo' and sniffed. "Oh, my! That smells delicious! Oh, you are so going to be used," she said, then pulled the shower knob and indulged in the floral scents and creamy textures of the homemade products. It was only when she noticed that the water was getting cooler that she realized the hot water heater was running low. "Oops! Time to get out and face the real world."

After she dried off and sampled the lotions and talcum powders, Kizzie felt recharged. All she needed was real food and at least five hours of uninterrupted sleep, and she'd be back to one hundred percent human. The eighty percent level she was at now was good, but she couldn't help but want more, especially since she could almost taste the aroma of dinner now that it was out of the oven.

And then she heard it—Zoe was giggling.

She'd laughed before. She was generally a happy baby,

but she was downright having a giggle fest, her squeals of joy rising and falling as she caught her breath, ready to start all over again.

"You like that ball, don't you?" the deep male voice asked. "Here you go. Now you throw it to me."

Kizzie inched her way down the stairs, her head poking around the corner to spy on her daughter's source of glee without distracting the entertainer. She could listen to that laugh all day and never get tired of it.

A dark-skinned man with a very short haircut had a red golf ball in his hand and was trying to get Zoe to grasp it. Although he had on black sweats and a neon orange long-sleeved tee shirt, he had the crisp, clean-cut appearance of a soldier. Holding the ball with one finger and a thumb, he was showing the little blonde baby how to grasp the fascinating red orb.

"You did it, Zoe!" he exclaimed when she bent her fingers around it.

Her giggles and squeals began again, her arm lifting up, fingers wide open again.

He put the ball back in her hand and renewed his efforts. "Now throw it," he said, and guided her hand, letting go at the last second so she would drop it.

"You did it again!" he said, then clapped his hands together. "Let's say yay!" he said and held her hands to show her how to clap.

"She can clap by herself," Kizzie said, then came down the stairs, glad that she was at least clean and presentable, even if all she had left to wear was an oversize UAA sweatshirt and drawstring pants with a hole in the knee. "I never thought to teach her the word for it, though. She's my first child and she's special needs. She...um...has Down Syndrome."

"Hi, I'm Heath," he said, standing up to shake Kizzie's hand. "And, just for the record, I believe all children have special needs. It's why it's called special: they're all different. Zoe's adorable." He glanced back at the walker Zoe was seated in, then turned and took the red golf ball. "No, no, honey. That's not for your mouth." He put the ball in his pocket then lifted her up out of the walker. "She really likes red. Or maybe it's the ball."

"I think it's you she likes," Kizzie said, then blushed as she realized that what she had said sounded like a flirt. "I mean, she doesn't act this way with her father..." Her face reddened even more. "I mean, I think dinner's ready, right? I'm so hungry, my brain has gobbled up all my common sense."

Bea came out of the kitchen with another place setting. "Heath, you're staying for dinner," she said rather than asked. She scowled as she searched for a place to put the plate down, finally deciding that at least one person would have to sit at the kitchen counter.

"Begging your pardon, Mrs. Zaharis, but I just came by to drop off these golf balls to your husband. Tell him I'm sorry I'll miss this week's game, but I'll be back on the 25th. I have a few things I have to tend to at Eielson, but I'll be ready to either meet or beat his handicap the first Saturday after that."

"You play golf in the snow?" Kizzie asked.

"Yes, ma'am, we do. That's why we play with red balls. Not that it makes the ball any easier to hit..." He glanced at Bea, rolled his eyes and shook his head. "Your dinner smells delicious, but I have a flight to catch. I might just plan to show up at supper time when I come back on the 25th."

Bea picked up the dinner plate and serviceware from the counter, ready to return them to the kitchen. "I'm counting on it. It may get elbow to elbow at the table, or even elbow to kitchen counter, but I always make enough food for friends and family. You're both. Now, if I can't interest you in dinner, at least I know you'll have room for something else. I made a few pocket-sized pies, just right for a plastic container. Stay still a minute…"

When Heath turned toward the door, Kizzie told him, "You'd better not sneak out of here. She'll chase you down like a little red golf ball in the snow."

"Just grabbing my jacket," Heath said. "Besides, I'll bet her slice is meaner than her drive."

"You got that right," Bea said, and handed him a paper bag with his to-go dessert. "Have a safe flight. Peace to you and yours and in all you do," she said, then gave him a big hug.

"Yes, ma'am," he said, then sighed at her scowl. "Thank you, Bea. Those words really do mean a lot."

"I know," she said.

"Mama, I'm hungry…" hollered a young voice.

"You'd better go feed the next generation of America's finest," Heath said, then pulled the knit cap out of his jacket and pulled it on. "Oh, and I'll remember to look for those special lotion recipes for you."

"Bless you all over again," Bea said, then held the door for him.

She shut the door behind him. "Such a nice young man," she said to Kizzie, then covered her frown with a phony smile. "Let's eat, folks!"

Kizzie picked up Zoe and sat down at the end of the table where she'd have room for her daughter on her lap.

"Why didn't you put her in the high chair?" Bea asked. "I set it up for her."

"I thought that was for Benny."

"I got the booster seat!" Benny crowed.

"Yeah, and I got the bicyclopedia," Robbie added. "That's a fat book Mama said has old stories in it."

"And I'm a big girl and don't need anything to sit on 'cept my bottom," LuLu said, her head held high, trying to make herself look taller and older than her six years.

"Okay. I'll try the high chair. I've never been able to get her to stay upright, though." Kizzie approached the seat as if it was a trash can she was supposed to toss her daughter into, leery of her weak-muscled daughter being able to support herself.

"Oh, you'd better use this, too, if she still slips sideways," Bea said. She brought out a bright yellow and orange flowered piece of fabric.

"An apron?" Kizzie asked, watching Bea slip it over the back of the high chair, spreading the ties off to the side.

"Nope. Just set her in there, the cloth between her legs…that's right." Bea brought the fabric with the ties up the rest of the way between the baby's legs, then tied a bow at the back of the chair, supporting the baby in an infant keep-her-upright straight jacket.

"Wow! I've never seen anything like that. If this works, I'll be able to have my bread and butter it, too!"

"Stick with me, Kizzie," Bea joked, "I'll show you more tricks than a seven-toed cat has toenails."

"Does that include how to make your bath toiletries? Those bath bombs were the bomb! And the shampoo and lotion…" She brought her hand up and sniffed the back of it. "Ahh…"

"I took some of my great-grandmother's recipes and modified them with botanicals from around here. Just about every neighborhood has at least one house with a lilac tree out front. I harvested as much as I could last spring with the older kids helping me and little Tommy stowed in a backpack. I have a few dandelion recipes I want to try out this spring. Maybe you and Zoe can help us with the harvest."

"Thanks. I could use the diversion. I didn't get a chance to tell you, but Butch is gone. Again. He signed up for another tour. I thought he was going to take a few classes, so he could get a promotion and stay stateside. At least, that's what he always told me. I think he'd rather do anything than spend time with us." Kizzie huffed in disgust, then took a big bite of roast beef dipped in mashed potatoes, stuffing food in her mouth so her foot wouldn't fit. *Bea doesn't want to hear your problems. Work it out with Butch, not the major's wife, no matter how nice she is.*

"Hi, honey. Sorry I'm late," Zeke called out as he hung up his overcoat on the hook in the mudroom.

"I know how it goes, an officer's work is never done," Bea said. "No need to apologize, but thanks just the same."

"No," he said, and bent to kiss her on her proffered cheek, "Major Zeke Zaharis knows how to delegate and defer tasks to a later time. The world will still turn in the right direction if I sign orders tomorrow, after I've enjoyed supper with my family and friends and had a good night's sleep. Thanks for joining us, Kizzie. And Zoe! My, how you've grown! Sitting in a high chair like a big girl, too."

He looked around the table, then back over to the

breakfast counter, the overflow diners' spot. "Where's Heath? I thought he was dropping by tonight."

"He was. I mean, he did. He said he had to go up to Eielson for a few days. He apologized for missing this week's golf game, but said he'd tangle with you on the first Saturday after the 25th."

"Oh. All right…" Zeke looked around, a frown of concern momentarily graying his face. "By the way, did he…"

"Yes, he did. He brought a whole box of red golf balls for you. Although, you might be one short. He may or may not have returned the one he and Zoe were playing with. Robbie, quit squirming and eat your dinner. We have pie for dessert."

"So, Kizzie, how's Butch adjusting to being back in the States?" the major asked, piling mashed potatoes on his plate.

Kizzie made the bite she had just taken last a long time, chewing as she thought of a diplomatic way to answer him. *Screw it! Quit protecting your husband! He made his own decision without consulting you—he can darned well pay the price of his actions.*

"The short version," she said, "is he's not."

"Not what?" the major asked.

"Not adjusting, coping, whatever you want to call it. We spent a little time together, then as soon as Zoe got a little fussy, he couldn't wait to leave."

"Oh, I'm sure he'll be fine..." he added a few pieces of meat and two ladlesful of gravy to his mashed potato volcano then decided he needed more gravy.

"No, I don't think so. He said he re-enlisted for another tour." Kizzie bit her bottom lip, willing herself not to cry, but it didn't work. Tears ran down the outside of her cheeks as she calmly said, "He said he'd be back in eighteen months. Maybe."

And then the waterworks let loose. "Oh, shoot," she said, holding the dishcloth to her face. "This was supposed to clean up Zoe's messy face, not mine." She took a couple of deep breaths, then guzzled half a glass of water. "I didn't set out to be a single mom, but if he doesn't want to be a part of our lives, I won't force him. Nothing's going to happen while he's deployed—like a divorce—will it?"

Zeke's fork stopped inches from his mouth, then he set it down on his plate. "I want you to continue being the good person you are. If Butch doesn't toe the line, he'll find himself missing more than a good woman and beautiful daughter.

Don't worry about him. He's a big boy and if he hasn't learned the importance of family…" He looked around at his family, Bea feeding the baby his last bite of food, his daughter and older sons scooting the peas around the potatoes on their plates, trying to make it look as if they'd eaten more food. "Well, the man's more than one shell short of a magazine."

"Mama," Zoe said, reaching for her mother's hand.

"She said mama!" Kizzie squealed, her face bright with joy. "That's her first word—mama!"

"March fourteenth, a day to remember," Bea said. "The day she said her first word and you stopped worrying about pleasing a man who could never be pleased. Now, see if she wants more of those potatoes, then I'm going to clear the table. March Fourteenth—3.14— is Pie Day and Pi Day!"

Chapter 2

June 15th
Near Anchorage, Alaska

"I'm sure glad it's green again," Kizzie said.

"You won't be when you're mowing the lawn every other day," Bea replied. "Of course, the neighborhood boys are happy about it. The months of April and May with no snow to shovel or grass to mow are tough on their spending money. Just teaches them to manage it more efficiently."

Kizzie knelt down and snipped the heads off the dandelions at the edge of the sidewalk and added them to the satchel slung at her hip. "Or they learn to get more creative in getting their parents to buy them what they want."

"I don't think the parents on post are as easily swayed, but then again, my tribe is still pretty young," Bea said, and subconsciously patted her belly.

"Oh, no. Not again?" Kizzie said before she could think. "I mean, congratulations! I'm sure LuLu is ecstatic."

Bea turned to make sure her six-year-old daughter hadn't picked up on their conversation. She hadn't. She was still trying to get Zoe to grasp the twisted nylon teething rope. "Unless someone gets reassigned, you'll have LuLu around to be Zoe's big sister for at least seven more months. Zeke isn't planning on retiring for a long time and his contract is good at JBER for another year or so. How about you?"

"Me? More children? I'd have to be exposed first. Butch was here for a whole week before he got ticked off and left. He was drunk for the first two days he was back. He knew I wouldn't have anything to do with him if he was plastered. At least, he pretended to be drunk. I caught him gargling with whiskey and spitting it out, dribbling some of it on his shirt so he'd reek. I called him out on it the next morning when he supposedly had a hangover…another excuse not to be intimate. Nope. We're over and done with—everything but the paperwork, I suppose. He doesn't call or write. His checks are always direct deposited, but he pulls out half right away. I make do…"

"Oh, he is so busted if he's not taking care of his family."

"On paper, he probably is. I haven't done anything 'wrong' except birthed a daughter he didn't want. I'm glad I wasn't tested when I was pregnant, or he would have bugged me to get an abortion. Nope. Even if I had known she had Down

Syndrome, I would have had her and loved her as much as I do now. Shoot! I love her all the more. I have to! She only has one parent..."

And then Kizzie broke down, tears streaming, nose running, shoulders heaving.

"Are you okay?" young LuLu asked, holding Zoe close to her chest so the baby wouldn't see her mother crying.

"Yes," Kizzie said, wiping her face with the back of her hand. "I just cut myself. It didn't break the skin, but it sure hurt. Sometimes the owies that don't bleed hurt the most. Tears can make you feel better, so don't ever be afraid of them, all right?"

"Okay..." LuLu said with a frown of uncertainty. "But be careful."

"Yes, sweetheart. I'll be more careful," Kizzie said, finding an honest smile to share at the unconditional love of a young girl. "Thanks for the warning. How about if we take a break for lunch? I feel like a hamburger and fries. How about you, Bea?"

"Um, not for me. My tummy's been a bit queasy lately," she said, and rolled her eyes.

"Huh?" Kizzie asked, then remembered Bea had said she

was in the early stages of pregnancy. "Oh, yeah... That's right. They have salads and I'm sure they'll give you extra soda crackers if you ask," she said.

"Sounds good to me. One last romp for these kids on the indoor playground after lunch and then we can all take a long nap."

"Speak for yourself and the kiddos. I have to see if I can find a job. I'm stretching dollars as best I can, but between food, gas, and diapers, I really shouldn't even be buying lunch."

As soon as the words were out of her mouth, Kizzie regretted them. "Don't mind me; I'm just whining. It's not that bad. I still have a few bucks left from our PFDs. I hate to touch her savings account, though. I mean, the Permanent Fund Dividend is supposed to be for something special, not for pull ups and baby wipes." She looked at her curly-haired daughter, all smiles and drool, another bib soaked. "I guess she won't be needing it for a college education, but I'd love to go somewhere special with her when she's old enough to remember it."

"Then make a plan. Set a destination and a year. Life is always much more satisfying when you have a goal you're working for." Bea held up her basket of dandelion blossoms. "Even if it's to gather a whole basket of weed blooms for making homemade botanicals."

"All right, Zoe. When you're six years old, we're going to Disneyland!" She picked up her daughter and grabbed the blanket she had been sitting on and threw it over her shoulder. "Come on, boys and girls. It's time for chicken nuggets and fries. The last one to the car has to empty the trash for everyone else."

"Wow!" Bea said, bringing young Tommy over her shoulder. "The way you wrangle these kids, you'd be a great daycare provider."

"Now, there's a thought… Maybe I can get a job doing that. At least, I'm pretty sure I could manage to bring Zoe to work with me if I had the right boss."

"Or you were your own boss. Never discount being the lady in charge. Even if it's bossing a bunch of snot-nosed, diaper-wrapped toddlers."

"Right… Meet you there."

***

"What happened? I thought you were right behind me?"

Kizzie asked.

"I was until Tommy decided to drop a load. At least, he's smiling again. Here, can you watch him while I go wash my hands?"

"Sure, that's why I have two knees. One for each toddler."

Bea glanced over at the two priggish women in the booth, their faces leaned forward as they whispered loudly to each other, their words caustic and clear. She followed their line of sight to see who they were talking about, then gritted her teeth. Now was not the time to do or say anything, especially since she knew she was on the hormonal roller coaster of pregnancy. If she even shook her head at the women in admonishment, she'd come unglued.

The two women were done eating when she came back, dumping their trash in the garbage. "I'd sure hate to have his job," the last one said as she walked out the door.

Bea clenched her jaws, her face scarlet by the time she got back to Kizzie and the children.

"What's wrong with you?" Kizzie asked.

"I'll tell you after we've ordered, when the older kids are in the play area. I'm afraid I'll say a very bad word. Grr!" Bea blew out a lungful of frustration and anger, then reached in her coat pocket. "Would you order three chicken nugget kids meals with fries, chicken salad for me and, what the heck, go ahead and get chocolate milks all around. Get whatever you want for you two and put it all on this." She set her debit card on the table and reached for her son. "My treat."

"But..."

"Before you say a word, you'd do it for me if our places were switched, right?"

"Yes, but..."

"No buts about it. Give me your little one, too." She hugged both two-year-olds close. "Suddenly, I'm exhausted."

Kizzie came back with two high chairs and her little plastic tent number. "I'm sure glad Zoe can sit up by herself now. She's happy with whatever I set in front of her, whether it's a toy or a metal ring from a canning jar." She reached for Tommy and put him in the other high chair. "Now, tell me what happened. You were so riled up, I thought you were going to shoot porcupine quills out of your eyebrows at those women."

"It's Heath. I saw him leave out the side door just as we came in."

"Yeah, and..."

"They were making snide comments about him being the Grim Reaper."

"What? Why would they say that? He's not old or ugly or…" Kizzie shook her head and frowned, confused.

"You don't know what his job is, do you?" Bea asked, then reached in her purse for the baggie of graham crackers. "Here you go, honey," she said, giving Tommy a cracker, then offering one to Kizzie for Zoe.

"The only time I ever met him was at your house late last winter," she said, holding the cracker for Zoe to nibble on. "He was pretty much leaving when I came in, although he did impress me. He had such a calm and caring demeanor. Zoe took to him right away. Actually, she likes most people, but *he* wasn't afraid of her. Folks generally back away or ignore her when they first see her. I guess she makes them feel uncomfortable or embarrassed or something."

"Well, he's a captain. A chaplain," Bea said. "It's his duty to give the bad news to wives—or husbands—when their spouses have been killed in the line of duty. Or otherwise, too, I guess. Those witches were saying, 'You don't want to see him at your front door' and 'At least, on any day but Sunday.' Hmph! Would they rather get the bad news on a sticky note on the windshield of their car?"

Bea picked up the nutritional information card and fanned herself with it. "Sorry. I do get riled up sometimes, but when I'm pregnant, it's worse."

Kizzie looked up and saw the server was waiting for Bea to finish her conversation before setting down the tray of food. "The chaplain's a real nice guy," the young man said. "And he even drops bills in the tip jar, not just pennies and nickels. Can I get you ladies anything else?"

"Yes, would you get me a couple extra packages of crackers?" Bea asked, taking the one off the tray and opening it with her teeth. "For some reason, I'm extra hungry today."

"Mommy, Mommy," Lulu cried. "Is lunch ready or can we play a little while longer?"

"Give me a few minutes to eat my lunch, then tell your brothers they get to have chocolate milk today. But wait until I'm done. How about I give you the signal?"

LuLu raised her fist in the air and pumped it. "Hoo! Hoo!" she said.

"That's my girl. My little champion." Bea stabbed her plastic fork into a piece of chicken and a cherry tomato.

"Now, go have fun for a few more minutes. I'll give the signal when I'm done."

"Hoo! Hoo!" LuLu answered, her fist stabbing the air. "Follow the leader and I'm the leader," she called out to the kids in the play area.

"First-borns are usually leaders as are big sisters. Looks like she would have been the boss, no matter what, though," Kizzie said, suddenly sad that her daughter would never be that bold or independent.

Bea saw the look of disappointment. "Yes, but LuLu was never as mellow or cuddly as Zoe. Every child is special— different in his or her own way. She eats, she sleeps, she breathes, she smiles. What more could any mother ask?"

"A husband who was glad she could do all those things," Kizzie said and sighed. She picked at her salad, found a piece of spoiled lettuce, took it out and set it aside. "You take the good with the bad, pull the rotten away so it doesn't spoil everything else, and then go on with life. I guess that's what I'll have to do next: get rid of the rotten."

She put the plastic lid back on the salad, her appetite gone. "I hate to say it, but I suppose I'll have to talk to his commanding officer about him taking the money out of the bank account. He doesn't have any need for it over there. He's just being a jerk. Shoot! His family is loaded. He has a trust fund set up by his grandfather, too. The only reason he joined the army was he had a college degree and knew he'd be an officer right off the bat. Plus, he thought he looked hot in a uniform."

Bea finished chewing, set down her fork, then held Kizzie's hand. "All that doesn't matter. Even his taking the money can be fixed. What I want to know is, do you love him?"

Kizzie thought for a moment, making sure she didn't give the reflex answer, the one that would come right from her gut. She shook her head very slowly, then increased until it was an absolute 'no.'

"I fell out of love as soon as he saw that Zoe was different. 'She's not mine,' was the first thing he said. 'But if she was, I'd tell you to send her away. You should have had the test so you could have had an abortion. She shouldn't have been born.'

"I cried and I cried and then the doctor came in and talked to me. He said her heart was strong. Her big toe and little toes had a space between them, but that was normal for many Down Syndrome children and shouldn't adversely affect her. Her eyes were crossed, but that happened with just about every newborn. Only time would tell if they would stay that way. Like other DS babies, her mouth was relatively small and tongue oversized, so if I would nurse her rather than bottle feed her, it would be best for her not just nutritionally, but for holding her tongue correctly and learning to swallow.

"And that's when I knew she was mine. She needed me. As soon as he said, 'nurse her,' my breasts got all tingly. We were separated by air now—no longer sharing the same circulatory system—but we were still one. We needed each other.

"I tried explaining it to Butch, but he wouldn't have anything to do with her. All he could think of was himself. 'What am I going to tell my parents? That I got a defective kid and you won't get rid of it?'

"And then he started in on how it couldn't be his child. He wanted a paternity test. I was ticked at first, indignant that he'd even think that. Then I figured, 'What the hell?' Get the test, rub it in his face. It was just as much his fault as mine. Then I calmed down. It was no one's 'fault.' It just was. She was different. She was special. But like Heath told me last winter, 'All children are special.' LuLu is special because she's so dynamic. Your boys are special, too. Shoot, I'm special. And I'm not going to let some creep who'd rather be half-way across the world, making molehills out of mountains with artillery because he doesn't want to be near his wife and not-his-idea-of-perfection child, make me feel bad. Screw him! We can and will have a life of our own."

Everyone in the restaurant stood up and applauded Kizzie as she finished her impassioned declaration of devotion to her daughter. Her family.

"Sorry to interrupt your lunch there, everyone," Kizzie said, her face scarlet, heart pounding. "I get a little wound up sometimes." She looked at Bea. "Can we take the kids home and have them eat their lunch there?"

Bea's answer was to stand up and give the signal. "Hoo! Hoo!" she hollered, then sat down. "The meals are already bagged. All we need to do is pile the kids into the cars, and we're outta here."

She reached over and patted Kizzie's hand. "You're awesome, lady, and I'm glad you're my friend. Butch is a jerk and doesn't deserve you. If I thought there was any 'saving' him from himself, I'd say get counseling. This goes deeper, though. Save yourself and Zoe. You need to cut him out of your life before he destroys your spirit or Zoe's or both. Any good man would be blessed to have you as a wife. And a good man would love Zoe, too."

"Finding another man is the absolute last item on my bucket list. I'm going to gain my freedom, get a job, and then Zoe and I are going to Disneyland!"

Chapter 3

"Good morning, Kizzie. How are you doing today?" Bea asked, calling on speakerphone so she could feed Tommy his oatmeal while talking.

"Meh. So, so. I came home and got out our wedding album and the shoe boxes of photos I've been going to organize for three years. I looked through them for about an hour, sometimes crying, sometimes laughing. Then I noticed something and went back through and looked at the pictures again. Butch was never looking into my eyes. It's as if he was checking his surroundings, making sure everything was ideal, holding his jaw perfectly parallel to the ground in a practiced pose. I never thought of myself as a token wife, but I guess I was. I don't even want to think that he was after my dad's money. I know he was in shock when he found out he had left it all to cancer research and that all I was to get was $10,000 toward my wedding. 'She's yours to take care of now, son. Make me proud.'"

"Do you think he did? I mean, make your dad proud before he died?" Bea asked.

"I don't know. He said that before the actual wedding. I think Butch joined the army because Dad had been active duty in the First Gulf War and he wanted to impress him. That and he liked the way he looked in a uniform. He wanted to make sure he was an officer before we were married. Once he was in, it was as good a job as any. He wasn't a self-starter and needed someone to tell him what to do. At least someone besides his wife. He didn't care for that."

"Is that why he asked to be assigned to Iraq? Because of your dad?"

"Actually, I asked him why he volunteered to go overseas. We had only been married a few months and I had just found out I was pregnant when he said he was being deployed." Kizzie shook her head, trying to erase the image of the shouting match that had ensued after she found out he had lied about being deployed when he had said it, but later called in a few favors to get reassigned overseas rather than stay on post. That should have been her first clue that he didn't want to be around a baby, 'normal' or otherwise.

"Kizzie, are you okay?" Bea asked. "No, scratch that. I know you're not. Just listen to me for a minute. The reason I called is I talked to my husband. Zeke says to talk to Butch's commanding officer first about the money problem. They don't treat divorces lightly and will make sure both of you have been through marriage counseling before any paperwork even gets started. I don't expect you two will reconcile, though. I'm just giving you the basic road map. It isn't an easy trail, and will take a long time, but you'll have to follow every step or have to start all over again at mile post one."

"Hmph. It's just a process, like making a souffle. No shortcuts. In the meantime, I think I have a line on getting certified for daycare. I'll keep you in the loop, just in case I need referrals."

"Kizzie, if they ask, I'll give you a five-star reference. Just take care of you and that baby. And if you need anything, make sure you ask. You'd want me to do the same, I'm sure."

"You know, you keep saying that, Bea, and honestly, it's the only reason I *do* keep asking. You're keeping me sane and humble, and I appreciate it."

"Watch out, though. When this next child comes, I might just be filling up your new daycare facility with my oldest four."

"Daycare facility?" Kizzie asked, then chuckled. "You're

sure aiming high for me, aren't you?"

"One of us has to. I'll catch up with you later. I think Tommy just gave me another present. That boy and his oh-so-efficient digestive system!"

"Later, then." Kizzie said and hung up. "Now what am I going to do? Do I really want the stigma of being a divorced woman?"

"Mama," Zoe called, her arms reaching up.

"Better to be a divorced, single mother than one with two babies to look after, one a six-foot six-inch narcissist. What in the heck are you doing with all your money, Butch? Four months in a row and every cent pulled out of the bank. Something's rotten in Iraq and it's more than the insurgents."

***

"Hey, Butch, you coming to the game tonight?" Wilson asked, a toothpick sticking out of the corner of his gapped-tooth grin.

"Nah, I thought I'd stay here and write a letter to my girlfriend," Butch said, his gut wrenching at the thought of how much money Wilson had managed to get off him since they'd been stationed together.

"Don't you want to try and get back some of that bonus money you lost last night? I thought for sure you would." Wilson nudged Butch's shoulder with a cold beer. "Lots more of these at the game," he said. "Non-stop beer is included in the ante. Coldest beer in Iraq. Guaranteed."

Colonel Peterson pulled back the bent fabric-covered door and stepped inside the tent. "Lieutenant Wadsworth, I'd like a word with you," he said, then glanced around the ill-kempt canvas structure. "Ten minutes. In my office," he said, then added brusquely, "And clean yourself up first. This place stinks like a barn. You can take care of your quarters after we have words."

"Sir. Yes, sir," Butch said, and both he and Wilson saluted the colonel.

Wilson picked up the beer he had hastily set behind the pile of laundry on the floor beside Butch's bunk. "Well, that didn't sound good…"

"No shit, Wilson." Butch looked around the broken-down living quarters he had resorted to after he had gambled away his living allowance, too. The salvaged tent from the decommissioned supplies depot was marginal accommodations, at best. He sniffed the air. It really did reek.

"Get out of here, Wilson," Butch grumbled. "And I won't be coming to your game tonight. I gotta get cleaned up for the colonel. Don't bother coming back here, either. I'm done with you and your crooked games…"

"Now watch what you're saying, Butch. You're the one who can't say no. I run an honest game. Lots of others manage to come out ahead. You just like the long shots a little too much," Wilson said, then gulped the rest of his beer. He crunched the can on his knee, then tossed it in the corner with all the other empties. "Come by when you're done with the colonel. I'll keep a six pack on ice for you."

"Get out!" Butch hollered. "Now!"

"All right, all right. You white boys are so excitable…" he said, then left the same way the colonel had, lifting the bent frame door up so it would swing out. There was a reason the tent had been scrapped. Too bad Butch was just as much a mess. One was usable, functional. Butch? Not so much.

***

"Parker, go see why Lieutenant Wadsworth hasn't come to see me yet. I gave him ten minutes half an hour ago," Colonel Peterson said.

"Sir. Yes, sir," Sergeant Parker replied, then walked out of the former luxury hotel that was now US Army headquarters, bypassing the officer's quarters where Butch should have lived to head to the dump.

Parker knew where to find Butch. She always listened to the gossip and rumors. It was part of her job as company clerk to know what was happening both on and off the radar. Butch always took his officer's housing allowance as cash. Three months ago, he had scavenged an old metal-framed tent to live in at the edge of the forward operating base, downwind from the dump. The aluminum and canvas structure afforded protection from the frequent sandstorms but didn't have facilities. Rumor had it that he had dug a latrine behind it and that he showered at the enlisted men's barracks once a month—as he said, whether he needed it or not.

Lieutenant William Wadsworth III—called Butch by just about everyone—was a gambler. Not a casual, 'Friday night win or lose a hundred bucks' kind of poker player, but a 'get rich quick on long odds at black jack and bet every dime and dollar you can scrounge' kind of jerk who'd yell and scream and blame everyone else for his losses guy: a total ass who

41

alienated everyone.

Parker pulled up to the tent, took one look at it, and tumbled out of the HMMWV and puked.

There was no mistaking the starburst pattern of the brownish-red color seeping through the tent wall.

Butch had bit a bullet.

Parker wiped her mouth and called it in. "We got another one, Gus. Lieutenant Wadsworth is gone. Send in forensics. There's no need for me to confirm it by looking inside. I'll head back to the office and start the paperwork."

***

"Thanks for coming on such short notice, Kizzie. I just went to the doctor and I'm bursting!"

Kizzie looked at Bea's belly. "No, you're barely showing. Actually, if I didn't know, I *wouldn't* know."

"No. I mean, did you know they can tell the gender at three months now? I'm having a girl! LuLu's finally getting a baby sister!"

"Oh, I'm so happy. Now we'll have three girls and three boys in the tribe," Kizzie said, her sincere smile fading as she realized that at any time, they could be pulled away from each other. Military moms were a close-knit bunch but were also at the whim of commanding officers and their orders changing.

"Don't look so glum. As I said, we're good for a while here. Besides, you need to enjoy what you have today and not worry about tomorrow. You can't change the future, no matter how much you worry about it, so don't!"

"Bea, I…I…I couldn't do it. I mean, I really don't want to be married to Butch, and I doubt he'll ever be a father—or rather, a daddy—to Zoe, but I can't start divorce proceedings on a guy while he's overseas. That's a pretty chicken-you-know-what thing to do. I'll just wait until he comes back…"

"Kizzie, you don't have to start proceedings, but you do have to talk with his commanding officer about him taking all the money."

"I'm sure something just came up… He'll start leaving it in again soon, I'm sure."

"How many months has it been?"

"He started taking half of his pay after he had been over there six months. Five months ago, he started pulling it all out, just leaving twenty bucks in the account so they didn't close it. It's still in there, so I guess I'm not *that* desperate,"

Kizzie said, then chuckled nervously. *Almost, but we'll see how far I can stretch beans and canned tomatoes.*

"Oh, he is so in trouble…"

"Please don't say anything, even to Zeke. Let me give him one more chance. I just wrote him a letter this morning, telling him how dire our circumstances are, asking him to let go of his anger and give us a chance." Kizzie reached into Zoe's diaper bag and pulled out the letter. "It's ready to go. I just need to get it to the post office."

"Let's celebrate the birth of another daughter first. How about helping me make a bunch of sugar cookies…with pink frosting!"

"How would you like that, Zoe?" Kizzie asked. "You can be the official taster!"

"Mama," Zoe said, then stuck her first two fingers in her mouth.

"I never tire of hearing her say that," Kizzie said. "And if she's teething again, at least she's not hurting. That's cause for a celebration, too!"

***

"Kizzie, would you help me clear out this freezer? I swear I was going to make pies before a new crop of peaches came out, but I don't think I'll be able to. Oh, and by the way, since I'm in a cleaning mood, I decided we need to have a summertime Thanksgiving dinner. I have a turkey in the freezer, too. I'll set it in the fridge tonight, so do you think you and Zoe can come by Saturday afternoon for a feast around 2:00? The turkey should be ready by three, but I want more time to chit chat. And make sure you bring all your leftover containers. I'm going to set you up!"

"Bea, you are so clever, but I can see right through you. You have to be the most generous…"

"You mean selfish. I don't want to have to deal with de-boning the turkey and emptying all the pots, making room in the refrigerator, listen to my family whine about having turkey *again* after the second or third time. Besides, if you clean up the turkey, I can play with the girls. I'm so excited!"

Chapter 4

Kizzie pulled up in front of the Zaharis home and called Bea from her phone. "We're here," she said. "I was just calling so you could maybe send LuLu out to help me bring in a few things."

"She's on her way."

"Whatcha need, Kizzie?" LuLu asked. "Do you want me to carry Zoe? I can, you know. I'm a big girl now. I'm seven next week!"

Kizzie finished unbuckling Zoe from her car seat and said, "What I'd really like is if you'd carry this in for me. I made peach pies!"

LuLu reached for the plastic handle on the pie carrier. "Just one?" she asked.

Kizzie snuggled Zoe close and grabbed her diaper bag, slipping it into the crook of her elbow. "Actually, I made several, but we don't need to bring them all in right now. We can make two trips."

"Would you like a hand?" Heath said. "Sorry to barge in. I just got here and overheard you. I'd be more than happy to carry this little princess in."

"Oh, my!" Kizzie gasped, surprise stealing her breath. "I didn't hear you drive up."

Heath chuckled. "That's because I walked over. I live two doors down. I lucked out. This is family housing, but the one-bedroom apartments were filled up. I'm here until they need a three-bedroom residence for a family. Right now, it looks like I'll be Bea and Zeke's neighbor for a while." He reached for Zoe. "May I? I'd rather hold this one than peach pies any day."

"Um, sure. She's already reaching for you."

"Mama," Zoe said, clutching Heath's ear, her face leaning into his Hawaiian print shirt to suck on a red hibiscus.

"No, I'm not your mama," Heath said. He gently relaxed her grip on his ear and turned her around, so she wasn't trying to eat the flower on his shirt. "There's your mama."

"You're the first one she's talked to other than me. She really doesn't babble much."

Heath lifted Zoe and checked her out like he was inspecting her. "She's what? Two years old? She'll start talking any day now. Mama's just the first of many words in this young lady's vocabulary. Pretty soon, you'll wish she'd never started!"

Kizzie shook her head. "Nope. I doubt that. I cherish all her achievements—each and every little milestone."

"Yup. Zoe is developing on her own schedule," Heath said, and nuzzled her cheek with the top of his head. "The Zoe calendar of life achievements is like no other." He turned back to Kizzie, blinking back moisture, and asked, "Is there anything else you need help with? I still have another arm."

The cardboard box with two pies in it nestled in her arms, Kizzie shut the car door. "Nope, we got it." She sniffed back the surprise tears at the glowing praise Heath had just shared. "I think I'm developing allergies," she said.

"Me, too," Heath said, and wiped away a tear that had escaped. *Such a sweet, sensitive mother. If only mine had been that wonderful, I'd still have my sister in my life.*

Bea met them at the door, young Tommy in her arms, shooing back rambunctious Robbie and Benny. "Keep back, boys. Let the folks come in. If you don't, the pie will be on the ground, not the counter, and you won't get dessert tonight."

Both boys scrambled to the corner, scattered with brightly-colored plastic trucks and building blocks. "Is this far enough?" Benny asked, his hands at his sides, pushing himself close to the wall.

"Kizzie, can I play with Zoe?" LuLu asked.

Kizzie looked at Heath, his focus on her daughter, oblivious to anyone else in the room or the activity that was suddenly all around.

"Why don't you let Heath play with her for a while? He hasn't seen her in months and you see her several times a week."

LuLu huffed an exaggerated sigh. "I guess so..."

Bea had been watching from the kitchen and decided a mini rescue was needed. "Yes, you're far enough away, Benny. And LuLu, would you come set the table, please?"

"Hoo, hoo," LuLu said without enthusiasm, her fist pawing at the air rather than punching it.

"And then you can decide which flavor of ice cream we'll have with the pie."

"Hoo! Hoo!" she hollered and punched the air with her usual vigor. "Peach ice cream with peach pie!"

"Hey, boys," Kizzie said as she walked up to the play area. "Can I come over and play with your blocks? I used to be pretty good at making bridges with these things. The trucks won't be able to drive on them, but they can sure go under them."

"Yeah, yeah," they chorused, happy to have Zoe's mommy's attention.

Ten minutes later, her colorful bridge and city walls complete, Kizzie looked back to make sure Zoe was all right. It had been ages since she had given her undivided attention to anyone but her daughter. Now that Zoe was weaned and before Bea had daughter number two, maybe she could have a few hours down time. She frowned as she realized that now that she had potential freedom, she didn't have any money, not even enough for gas for a trip down Turnagain Arm.

She glanced over at the diaper bag, the 'Dear Husband, please help out your wife and daughter' letter still poking out the side, her resolve never strong enough to take it to the post office.

"Can you wave to your mama?" Heath said, holding Zoe's hand. "Watch this," he called out to Kizzie.

He let go and Zoe's hand kept waving, the smile of accomplishment on her face just as broad and bright as the one on Heath's.

"Oh... That's so precious," Kizzie gushed, then got up and

took her daughter out of his arms.

"Another one for the Calendar of Zoe," Heath said, then rubbed under his nose. "Danged allergies," he said, stifling another tear.

Kizzie wiped the corner of her eye, the same liquid joy spilling out. "Yeah. Me, too."

"Dinner's ready," Zeke called out. "I think we'll have to start a new tradition. A second Thanksgiving dinner on the first Saturday after the summer solstice. That should be easy enough to figure out."

"Oh, and Heath, remind me to show you something after dinner," Bea said. "I had my sister do a little digging in some church records. The internet might be good for researching some things, but when it comes to family heritage, not much can beat church records."

"You got that right," Heath said. "No matter if they're Catholic, Protestant, Jewish, Mormon, or Muslim: family births, deaths, and other rites are meticulously recorded and preserved by the church or temple. I won't let you forget to show me, that's for sure. I've been waiting for new intel for years! Now, where do you want me to sit?"

"Either side of a high chair or booster with a child in it. This time around I figure we have enough adults to help feed all the babies. Why didn't I think of this before?" Bea set small bowls of mashed potatoes and peas in front of each child. "All I'm missing is a canine vacuum for spillage."

"Just say when on that, Bea. Recently deployed soldiers are coming to me all the time, wanting to know if I know of anyone who wants a dog—a good, well-behaved dog that won't be able to go overseas. In the meantime, may I offer a prayer?"

"I was just going to ask you to do the honors, Heath," Zeke said, and took his wife's hand, their arms behind Robbie.

"Lord, bless these families You have created that have become one. Keep us all safe, healthy, and aware that You have it all under control. Thank You for the food, the home, and the children who have graced our lives. May we be strong enough in You to share You with others. In Jesus's name, amen."

"Amen," everyone chorused except Zoe, who said, "Mama."

"You got that right, little one. Thank you for your mama and amen."

"Do you need help cleaning up?" Heath asked Bea when they were done, his gleam of excitement impossible to contain.

Zeke looked over and saw his golf buddy was busting at the seams of his colorful shirt with excitement. "Why don't you two take care of the church records while Kizzie and I clean up the kitchen. LuLu has the babies under control and the boys are doing a little re-engineering on Kizzie's bridge."

Crash!

"It's a good thing it's plastic. She can help them rebuild it later."

"You don't have to offer twice," Bea said, and dried her hands on her apron. "Come on into Zeke's study. There aren't any distractions in there."

Heath followed her into the room. Even though it was already brightly lit with natural light, Bea still flipped on the overhead light. "Here it is," she said, and pulled the manila envelope from between two books in the bookcase. She took out the single paper and handed it to him.

"Here, this might be better," she said, and handed him the magnifying glass from the top drawer.

"Shoot! I think that's her name, but the other information is so faded, I can't read it, even with this." Heath handed the magnifying glass back to Bea. "Is this my copy?"

"Yup. I don't need it for anything. She's not my sister. Go ahead and take it," Bea said, offering him the envelope. "I'd keep it in this, though, so the kids don't get their grubby hands on it. I think your presence is missed."

"Yeah, I hear the boys calling for Kizzie. I think the little Zaharis kingdom has selected its queen. Queen Kizzie: who would have thought? Maybe I can wrestle Zoe away from LuLu."

Bea walked back into the kitchen. "Okay, I'm back to help with clean up, Whoa! You got that bird picked clean in a hurry, Kizzie."

"And I'm not a slouch at packing up the potatoes and sides, either," Zeke said, pointing to the stack of leftover containers. He gave his wife a quick kiss. "The dishes practically loaded themselves into the dishwasher, so all that's left is to wipe off the table, chairs, and counter. Teamwork!"

"Hoo! Hoo!" Kizzie said and punched the air.

Heath grabbed the dishcloth from the sink and rinsed it

out. "I'll handle the final clean-up chores, you three. Go take a load off. I'm so grateful for this get together. Barbecues may be nice, but there aren't any mosquitoes inside."

Zeke looked up at the clock. "Since the sun's still shining, I was going to suggest a late nine holes after dinner, but I think I have tryptophan fever. Let's call it off until next week."

Heath patted his flat belly, trying to pouch it out but failing. "Me, too. Turkey and mashed potatoes will make me sleepy every time."

"And don't forget, we still have pie and ice cream," Kizzie called out from the rainbow block village that now surrounded her.

"And I have an announcement to make," Zeke added, his arms now around his wife, standing behind her to comfort her and his unborn daughter. He nuzzled her neck and rocked her back and forth. "It doesn't get any better than this. Good health, great friends, and peace. What more could anyone ask?" he whispered.

"What's that, Daddy?" LuLu asked. "Are we going to get a puppy to clean up the messes my brothers leave on the floor after eating?"

"Hmm." Zeke rubbed his chin, drawing out the anticipation

of his answer, all three boys now looking at him for the answer. "No. No puppies..."

"Awww," the children groaned.

"But we might see about getting one of the dogs that Heath was talking about. But that's just a maybe on whether we get one. And it will definitely be an older one and already potty trained. You see, if I'm going to have a new member of this house who isn't potty trained already, it's going to a real baby." Zeke looked at Bea and winked.

"I saw you wink at Mommy," LuLu said, then bounced up from the floor. "Does that mean we're having another baby?" she asked, her hands clutched together under her chin.

"Oh, boy! Another brother!" Robbie said, then high-fived Benny.

"No," Zeke said and looked into LuLu's wide eyes. "You're getting a sister!"

"A sister? Oh, boy! I mean, oh, girl! I'm getting a sister. My very own little sister." LuLu stopped suddenly, her exuberance gone as quickly as it had appeared.

She bent down to Zoe and picked her up from the activity quilt she had been playing with. "She might be my very own sister, but you'll always be the first sister I had, Zoe. You're mine forever."

Heath sniffed back the tears, then feigned a sneeze. "Darned allergies," he said.

Kizzie wiped her eyes and sniffed, too. "Yeah," she said. "Really." *I know why I'm fighting back the tears—what's your excuse, Heath?*

Chapter 5

Heath took pictures of the document in the bright sunshine and under fluorescent lights, with a camera and with a scanner connected to a computer that had the latest and greatest programs available to the public. He was just about ready to ask a favor of one of his parishioners in satellite surveillance when he tried adjusting the daylight photo with a free app he had downloaded. He cranked up the resolution and suddenly it was bright and clear: her birth date.

He was only five when his parents had given away his baby sister. "She's broken," they had told him. "We're taking her to a hospital where they can fix her."

"She's not broken! But if she was, when are they gonna give her back?" he cried.

He couldn't remember his exact words—just that he kept arguing that she wasn't broken, his parents telling him the hospital would have to keep her. He even bundled her up in a blanket, made her three bottles and put them in his backpack along with a few disposable diapers and ran away with her. He didn't get too far beyond the end of the driveway when they caught the two of them, but he was willing to run away and take care of his baby sister rather than let them give her away.

After she was gone, he wouldn't talk to them for months. Or so it seemed. He remembered praying out loud every night for her return. At least for a few nights. Finally, his father tired of hearing it. He came in and told him the Lord would take care of Willa, but that he couldn't pray out loud for her because it made his mother cry.

"Then she shouldn't have given her away! She wasn't broke. She was perfect! She was my sister!"

He didn't know which hurt most, the spanking for yelling at his father or seeing his father—the big and scary drill master sergeant—cry for the first and only time in his life. He did keep praying that Willa would come back, but he did it silently.

It was years before he could look either parent in the eye again, always wondering if they'd give him away next because he wasn't perfect. Because he was broken.

In retrospect, it drove him to be a better student, a harder practicing athlete and musician, always in the back of his mind worrying that he'd be sent away if he didn't meet their ideal standard. Would he be considered broken and given away if he didn't learn the scales on the piano the first week? Would he be tossed aside if he ever got less than an A on a report card?

His obsession got to be a habit, always striving for perfection, until he made a new friend. Jesse only stayed at the school for a year before his mother was transferred, but he reminded Heath of his sister. Their eyes were alike, his small mouth always ready to smile just like Willa's. Jesse was small for his age and a happy boy who liked to give hugs. Not everyone liked him. It wasn't because he ever did anything wrong—it was only because he was different. He wasn't broken, though. He was a perfect Jesse.

Tears fell freely as Heath remembered his friend. Jesse had his own teacher for all the other classes but joined the rest of the fourth graders for gym. The first time Jesse had given him a bear hug, he was embarrassed. No one ever chose him when they had to choose up teams, so the teacher assigned him to one group or another. The one time Heath got to be captain, he chose Jesse first and ignored the loud groans from his friends. He gave Jesse a thumbs-up and a smile, bestowing acceptance upon Jesse, a feeling the boy had never had when he was with the 'normal' kids.

It was just a game of field hockey. Nothing special. Not a field day or a track meet. Just the class that met on Tuesdays and Thursdays between one and two o'clock. Jesse had told him he and his mom practiced kicking the ball and he was real good at it. Whether he was or wasn't didn't make a difference to Heath: he was going to give him a chance.

His team was already ahead, but he didn't care whether they won or lost. He'd give Jesse his moment. He ran the ball down the field, calling to Jesse to keep up. The boy was smaller than the rest of the boys, but Jesse ran as fast as he could while Heath trotted, keeping pace with him. "Okay, now kick it," he said, and tapped the ball so it rolled in front of Jesse, just before they reached the goal net.

Jesse watched the ball come to him, then pulled back and kicked, a glancing blow, but still straight enough that it landed right in front of the goal. Heath motioned for him to finish kicking it in, then looked up at the opposing team. "Hey guys, watch this!"

And they did. All eyes were on Heath as he bowed to one side, his arm out to show off his companion, the break in the player's attention allowing Jesse time to kick the ball the rest of the way in and score the fifteenth goal of the afternoon.

The whole class roared with cheers for Jesse. Well, all except for the few who had already lost the match before Jesse took the kick.

"Yup, Jesse wasn't broke. Just different."

Heath jotted down the new information into the little journal of notes he kept on his sister—not that he'd ever forget her birthdate. He'd never known it, and now that both his parents were gone, he'd never have found out. The rest of their family wasn't close and those who he had found either didn't know he ever had a sister or didn't know her birthday.

"I'll find you one of these days, Willa. I need to give you at least one more hug. Or a million more. Just depends on whether you'll let me into your life or not. I shouldn't have let them give you away."

Chapter 6

"Here you go, sir. It's another one. I mean," the corporal stammered, as he handed Heath the large manila envelope. "It's another 'under investigation,' sir."

Heath knew what that meant. It was unofficial code for suicide. Too many soldiers lost their lives at their own hands. Was it the stress of separation, long hours, shock of the whole horrid war situation or something else? Maybe it was all of the above plus a few more. After years of research, no one had the answer. All he knew was he was going to have to speak to another spouse.

It was never easy, but the worst cases were the ones with children left behind. How could the young ones understand when the surviving parent couldn't? Or even the professionals?

His schedule was supposed to be forty hours a week, but when one of these came through, he'd give it his all. Or at least, all that the surviving spouse would allow. Sometimes it was a man who took his own life, less frequently a woman. Either way, he had to make sure the ones left behind didn't suffer from the rebound effect. The loss of a loved one was tough. So tough that the survivor felt that one life wasn't worth living without the other. The chaplain's job was to make sure that two lives weren't taken with one bullet.

Never leaving the widowed alone was the best way to ensure that didn't happen. He opened the soldier's file, searching for the name of the next of kin and address. He scanned it quickly and noticed there weren't any contacts other than the spouse and parents. If he had a network of friends, this William Wadsworth III didn't feel like sharing it with the army. He'd ask his CO in Iraq if the man had had friends in Alaska who could spend time with his wife. If not, the man was an officer. The women's auxiliary would see that Mackenzie Wadsworth had support, plenty of food, and a shoulder to cry on. They were great that way. Still, it would be nice if they didn't have to help, that suicides never happened, that soldiers—hell, anyone—never got so depressed that ending their lives seemed the only option.

"Corporal, you're coming with me," Heath said.

"But, but…" he protested.

"No buts about it. I don't like this anymore than you do. There has to be two of us and you're it today. When we're done here, I need you to contact the officer's wives' auxiliary and set them up with a schedule so Mrs. Wadsworth is never alone. Grab your hat and let's go."

When they drove up to the post housing, the corporal balked, his face ashen.

"Is there a problem? Do you know Mrs. Wadsworth?"

"No, sir. I'm just afraid…"

"Afraid of what? She's the one who has the burden, not you. You have a healthy life, a family, I presume, a future. She has mountains of paperwork, will have to move off post in a few months, which means dealing with finding new housing, maybe a job…"

"You're right, sir. I shouldn't have been feeling sorry for myself." He took a deep breath, then said. "I'm ready, sir. Let's do this."

"Now, don't get callus, either. It's a fine skill to be emotionally strong while being sympathetic."

"I'll do my best, sir," he said, then got out of the car.

"I can't ask any more than that, although it might help if you thought of her as a sister or a cousin. She's a real person with the world about to crash down on her shoulders."

Heath looked at the corporal, suddenly ashen. "And don't forget to breathe."

He took a deep breath and nodded. "Yes, sir."

Heath mumbled a quick prayer as he walked up to the front door, asking for the strength to last until the end of the month when his enlistment was up, for the strength to get through another day. He sighed and knocked on the door. For right now, the strength to get through the next five minutes would be enough.

He kept his eyes to the ground as the door knob turned, still timid about looking into the eyes of a woman who was about to hear the worst news of her life.

"Yes?" she said.

Heath looked up, recognizing her voice.

"Kizzie?"

"Oh, hi, Heath. I didn't recognize you in uniform and with your head down. Nope, your laces aren't untied and…"

Kizzie's knees buckled as she remembered the conversation at the fast food restaurant. 'You don't want to see him coming to your house in uniform.'

Heath rushed forward and took Zoe in one arm, supporting Kizzie with the other.

"Help me get her inside, Corporal."

The corporal maneuvered around Heath, overloaded with an unconscious woman in one arm, a baby playing with his ear in the other, and cleared a path.

"I take it you know her," the corporal said, "And the baby, too, it seems."

"Yes, we're mutual friends of Major Zaharis. I just had dinner with all of them this weekend. Go get me a glass of water from the kitchen."

The corporal looked around, found the kitchen, and came back with the water. "I dampened a dish towel for you, too, sir. Sometimes a cool cloth on the back of the neck helps revive them."

"Good thinking. You'll go far in a hurry. Here, take Zoe for a minute while I tend to the mother."

Okay, Lord. Help both of us, all three of us, get through this. I don't know the back story, but I've never heard her talk about a husband, so maybe they weren't close.

"Kizzie. Kizzie. Wake up." Heath leaned her forward so he could place the towel on the back of her neck. "Wake up, honey. I mean, wake up, Kizzie."

Kizzie's eyes popped open, but they seemed lifeless, staring without seeing. Even though she blinked, it was if she was in another world.

"Kizzie. Kizzie. You have to wake up."

Heath didn't say the words. Maybe if he doesn't say he's dead, he won't be. Maybe if I don't come back to the real world, all the horrors will go away. Maybe it was an accident and someone else was killed and they just thought it was Butch. Maybe a close call like that will make Butch quit being such a jerk and he'll love me again, love Zoe for the first time…

"Kizzie, you have to wake up for Zoe's sake. I know you don't want to hear what I'm going to say, and I understand that, but you have to be strong. Zoe needs you."

Kizzie gulped air, then coughed and started crying at the same time. "So, you're here to tell me Butch is dead?" she asked, her once vacant and dry eyes now flooded with tears and questions.

Heath took a composing breath and 'put on the suit,' assumed the role of bad news bearer, hiding his own persona under the shield he had devised for his own sanity years ago. "I'm here to inform you that your husband, William

Wadsworth III, has died. The circumstances surrounding his death are under investigation. We have resources on hand here on post to assist you in your time of mourning and transition." He reached into his inner jacket pocket and pulled out the flyer with the names and numbers of the service organizations and what their specialties were. "My phone number is on the back if you need help with prayer. The officers' wives' auxiliary will also be on hand to help you during this time."

"Heath, are you in there?" Kizzie asked, frightened by the alter ego that had taken over. "I think you're more messed up than I was."

Despite the direness of the circumstances, Heath had to stifle a chuckle. "At least I didn't faint," he whispered. He shook his head. "I didn't know it was you when I got the word that we'd lost another soldier. So, your name is really Mackenzie?"

"It was either that or Mac. Or Zee. Or Ken. Or...well, Kizzie fit me great when I was a toddler. I've grown accustomed to it now."

"Are you two all right?" the corporal asked.

"Yeah, I think we're both avoiding reality right now," Heath said. "It's safer. The ton of bricks will find us eventually, though. In the meantime, can I take you over to Bea's? It's not a good idea for you to drive anywhere for a few weeks, at least."

"What? Are they afraid I'm going to kill myself or something?" Kizzie asked sarcastically, a step down from the snide tone she had wanted to use.

"Actually, yes. Your emotions are going to be all over the place for a while."

"I think I read something about that a long time ago. Remind me what they are. Gently," Kizzie said, a smile sneaking in at the end.

"The stages of grief? Okay. The first stage is shock. I think you passing out and going all glassy-eyed on me would be classified as shock. Then there's denial. I think that's a bit of what we have going right now—both of us.

"Then there's anger. You'll want to rage at anyone or everyone for the loss. Then there's bargain, trying to find a way out of the situation. Short answer to that one: there isn't a way out. Still, it's part of the seven stages, so let's hope you slip through that one real fast."

"Like when I'm asleep," Kizzie said, then giggled nervously.

"Right… Then there's depression…"

"Heath, I think I did that one already. I sure hope I don't have to go through it again."

"Yes, you probably will, but I'm here for you. And Bea is, too, I'm sure. I don't know how much family you have or if you are or were close to William's family…"

"Butch. He was called Butch."

"Sorry. I know that's important to call a person by his chosen name, not his given name. Next to last is testing, which is where you're going to find a way out of the situation, a realistic one."

"Like getting a job? Getting a life?" she asked.

"Like getting your sense of humor back, getting Zoe in pre-school and maybe starting a career so you two can have an even more wonderful life than being separated from the man you loved for long periods of time."

Kizzie sneered as he gave his explanation of what came next. "I haven't loved him since Zoe was born and he denied her. I tried to get him to love both of us, but as soon as he saw she was different, he didn't care about either one of us.

Shoot! As soon as he found out I was pregnant, he couldn't wait to get out of the country. He's *unloved* Zoe her whole life and stopped loving me when he found out I was pregnant. That is, if he ever did love me."

"How could anyone not love you, Kizzie," Heath said, then blushed scarlet. He looked up to see if his corporal had heard. He hadn't. He was on the floor, playing with Zoe and her colorful blocks.

"Heath, you've shown Zoe and me more love in the last week than Butch did in three years, four counting the engagement period when I was so eager to get married."

"So, the last stage of grief is acceptance. It almost sounds to me as if you're taking the shortcut to the last step, Kizzie."

"Yeah, I wish. We both know that won't happen. I'll try to be happy with just spending a moment or three in all the other steps and taking a lifetime for the acceptance part. Since I'm not supposed to drive, would you call Bea for me and see if you can take us over there? Suddenly, I don't like being in this place anymore."

Heath took out his phone, looked at it, then paused before dialing. "Should I tell her what happened or do you want to?"

"Good Lord, no. I mean, yes, you tell her. I don't think I could do it. Knowing it is one thing; verbalizing it or telling someone else about it is another."

Heath put his hand on her shoulder, but before he could tell her what he wanted to share, she put her cheek on his hand. "I'm glad it was you at the door. I know you have a hard job, and I don't know how you do it, but you're good at it. Not too bad at reviving swooning women, either. But if I had to hear it from someone, I'm glad it was you."

Kizzie brought her head back up. "I'm sorry. I got carried away. You were going to say something?"

"I was going to say that part of what I do as a chaplain is to be there for the family. That is, if they want me. I know you have Bea, but I don't want you to ever be alone. The women's auxiliary will help, too. They're good about bringing food, keeping your house clean and laundry done, taking you shopping and appointments as needed…"

Kizzie smiled as Heath rattled off all the tasks and taskers, then looked over at her daughter playing with the corporal who was now trying to balance blocks on his head, causing Zoe to squeal with laughter. "You'd think this would be the rottenest day of my life, but it isn't. Butch is dead. I get it. We all die, soldiers as a group usually a little faster than most of us. Yes, it would have impacted me a lot more deeply if we had been truly, deeply, madly in love and he felt the same way about our daughter, but that wasn't the case. I have a lot to process, forms to fill out, a funeral to plan and…"

Kizzie broke down, crying, sniffling, shoulders heaving as she bent forward.

"What's wrong," Heath asked, his hand on her back, reining in the urge to hold her in his arms and rock her like a child. He handed her the box of tissues from the end table.

"I…I…I have to tell his parents," she said.

"No, you don't. I can and will do that," he said. *And if they give you grief, they'll have to deal with me!*

"They…they'll blame me for his dying. If he hadn't tried to impress me, he would never have joined the army and been killed in action. It's all my fault even if it was his idea to join, not mine. I even tried to talk him out of it, but no…"

Kizzie blew her nose and composed herself. She sat up straight and looked Heath in the eye. "They think Zoe's defective, too. They supported Butch in telling me I should give her away. I wouldn't do it. They've never even seen her. After the phone calls from his mother, I decided she didn't deserve to even see a picture of Zoe. Butch's dad is a blob of putty. Whatever his wife does, he follows right behind. Not a length of spine in his sniveling body."

Heath held up the phone. "Um, should I call Bea first? I can take you and Zoe over there and call the parents after you're all set up. No one else is going to tell them, so you don't have to worry about them hearing it from someone else. I'm the one who signs off on 'notification of next of kin.'"

Kizzie tossed her used tissue in the trash and got a fresh one to wipe her eyes. "I'll be just a couple minutes getting her diaper bag together and a few overnight things for me. I'll sleep on Bea's couch with the baby before I'll come back here." She looked around the room. "And when I do have to finally come back, would you come with me?"

"Kizzie, I'll do anything you ask."

A laugh snuck out, but she tried to catch it with the side of her hand anyway. "You know how long I've waited to hear a man tell me that?"

Heath laughed back at her. "No, but I have to tell you, I've never said that to another woman, with or without the name of Kizzie."

As soon as she was out of the room, the corporal scooted over to Heath, the baby still in his arms. "So, I take it you two know each other well?"

Heath shrugged his shoulder and took Zoe. "Hey, darlin'. Did you miss me?"

"Mama. Mama," she said.

"Um, I think she's a little off on the names," the corporal said.

"Nope. That's just Zoe-speak for I love you. Well, I love you, too, little darlin'. And we're going to take care of your mama for as long as she'll let us."

"Beggin' your pardon, sir, but it sounds to me like you're smitten."

Heath put his forehead on Zoe's. "I sure am," he said.

"I meant the other one," the corporal whispered, nodding toward Kizzie who had just come in the room.

Heath sat back and looked at Zoe then up at Kizzie, now gathering blankets and toys from the playpen. "Hmm. I don't know, but maybe you're right. The timing sure sucks, though."

"Talking like that and you bein' a chaplain," the corporal said, then laughed.

"Ah, yes, but I am a man, too. Come on. Let's see how much of this stuff she wants to take to Major Zaharis's place. Oops! I'd better call first."

"Yup, you're smitten!"

Chapter 7

"Oh, honey, I'm so sorry," Bea said, greeting her at the front door with open arms.

"I guess I'm back in—or still in—the denial stage," Kizzie said as she pulled out of the hug.

Bea stepped aside and walked toward the two men standing next to the official sedan. "I don't like to say it, Heath, but sometimes I hate to see you in uniform. It's one thing when you're performing a wedding, but this…"

Bea faltered, and Heath dropped the plastic bag with Zoe's blankets and toys and rushed to her side, his new task to comfort the comforter. "It's all right, it's all right…" he said. "He," he nodded to the sky, "has it all under control. What we need to do is make sure Kizzie and Zoe are taken care of."

He looked up and realized that both Kizzie and the corporal had disappeared. "Where'd they go?"

Heath stepped in the house and Bea peered around the corner. "I hear them now," she said. "They're playing with the children in the backyard. I'm so glad we got that enormous play set. Best investment in toys yet."

Heath nodded, then waited for Bea to look at him, letting her have one more smile of gratitude before he told her the rest of the story.

"Butch took his own life. The official report says, 'under investigation,' but that means suicide."

"Are you sure?" she asked, her face pale with shock.

"Come on inside. You need to sit down. This isn't going to affect the baby, is it?" he asked, looking down at her belly.

"No, she's okay. I felt her move last night. We'll be fine. It's those other two females I'm worried about. Scratch that. Zoe will be fine, too. She never had a relationship with her father. I don't know if he had even held her. But tell me, how do you know he took his own life? And why?"

"I have no idea on why he did, but he wasn't killed in action, he wasn't in a vehicular or any other type of accident, and there wasn't any mention of arrests or a person of interest being detained in association with the incident. I didn't know the man, so I can't grieve on a personal level for anything but the loss of a life in such a desperate manner. I can, and will, grieve with Kizzie for the changes she's going to have to endure in the next few months, though. I'm sure I can count on you to be her support."

"Absolutely! I just transitioned Tommy to a toddler bed with his brothers, so until this baby comes in six months, we have a spare room. I'm sure Kizzie will want to bunk with Zoe."

"There's no rush. She still has the house for a few more months. The army doesn't just kick the widow or widower to the curb right away, but she told me when she packed up that she didn't want to go back."

"That's understandable. She was there more without him than with him, but they were together when they first moved in. There had to be love at some time or another or they wouldn't have had a baby. Oops. Sorry, Heath. That was crude."

"I may be single, but I do know how babies are made," he said with a chuckle. "Let's go check on the crew. I don't know what comes next in this scenario. Each condolence case is different, but this is even more unique."

"Before we go, I know a few things about their relationship that I'm not at liberty to share, but just let me say that I think she's better off without him than with him. *Tsk!* Withdrawing all his pay and leaving her to scramble for food and diaper money." Bea's hand flew up to her mouth. "Oops! I said too much. Sorry."

"No, don't be sorry. That actually makes me feel better." He took off his hat and set it on the table by the door. "I have to stay in uniform, but I think I can get away without the topper. I don't want to frighten Zoe."

"Or Kizzie. The uniform is a reminder of why you came to see her. Make sure when you come by, you're wearing a tee shirt or even one of your colorful Hawaiian shirts. You're more than our friend to her. You're her friend, too. The man she admires, the man who adores her daughter."

And the man who adores her. I can't tell her that, though. She just found out she's a widow less than an hour ago. Telling her how I felt at this point would definitely be moving too fast!

Kizzie looked up from her position on the ground with Zoe between her legs. Bea and Heath were coming out to join her, the corporal, and the children on the rambling cedar and plastic playground. Phew! Heath had his hat off. He was 'at work' right now and had to be in uniform, but if she... She held her hand up in front of her face, blocking his starched and pressed dark suit from her vision. There, that was better.

"Is the sun in your eyes, Kizzie?" he asked.

"Nope, just blocking the glare of your official capacity. And please, don't ask me how I'm doing. I'm sure I'll hear that more times than I care to in the next few weeks. Shoot! The next few months and years. I gotta get a life and get out of this place."

She brought her hand back down to her side, then looked at the children, Bea's bunch either swinging on the bright yellow seats or sitting on the synthetic mat the play yard was set upon. "Or maybe I'll stay. I feel like I'm home here with all these kids. You may feel your calling as a chaplain, but I feel mine with shepherding the wee ones."

"If you'd like to know a little secret…" he said, then knelt down beside her. "My calling is being a shepherd, too. I don't need to be in the army to do that, either. I didn't re-enlist, so at some point in the near future, I'll be a civilian. A pastor looking for a flock."

"Oh, really," Kizzie said, her mouth hanging open at the unbidden thought of living the rest of her life as a pastor's wife. She quickly shut her mouth and sat up straight. "Oh, really," she replied again, a slight smile of hope and composure replacing her amorous shock. "That's going to be awesome."

"Are you and Zoe all right here for a while?

I…ahem…have another phone call to make."

Slam! Reality rears its ugly head. That means he needs to call Butch's parents. "We're fine. I really appreciate you calling them. We, um, don't have a very good rapport." Kizzie rolled her eyes, trying to make light of the absolute hatred Butch's mother had towards her. "I suppose I'll have to see her at the funeral services…"

And then it happened again. The tears pouring out, shoulders heaving uncontrollably. Meltdown number two.

"Uh, oh," Bea said, rushing to her side. "Let's go in the house for a minute, Kizzie. Heath, Corporal: do you have the kids under control?"

"No problem," the corporal said. "I have three of my own."

Heath picked up Zoe as Bea helped Kizzie to her feet. "There, there, honey. It's perfectly normal. It's going to happen when you least expect it. Let's go get a box of tissues for you…"

"Do you think she's going to be all right?" the corporal asked.

"She will if I have anything to say about it." Heath moved over to the adult-sized chairs in the shade and sat down, Zoe on his knee. "Let's play a Humpty Dumpty for a bit," he said, "while Mama lets Aunt Bea help pull her back together again."

I wish I could be the one at her side. Thirty losses I've had to deal with since I've been here, sixteen of them the result of suicides. Each one was just as miserable as the first, but this one is ripping my heart out. I hate to admit that I don't care about the man passing because that means Kizzie will no longer be married. If that's making me feel guilty, imagine how it would tear her up to have the same feelings?

"Humpty Dumpty sat on a wall," Heath sang as he bounced Zoe. "Humpty Dumpty had a great fall," he tipped her sideways, causing her to giggle at the change of direction. "All the king's horses, and all the king's men, couldn't put Humpty together again." *But if this King has anything to do with it, Kizzie will not only be healed, she'll be Mrs. Heath King!*

***

"Bea, I wasn't crying because Butch died or because there's going to be a funeral." Kizzie wiped her nose again, then took a deep breath, ready to admit the truth. "I cried for me. Because I'm the one left behind to deal with all the crap while he's spending eternity in hell or wherever. I'm the one who's going to have to deal with his mother. I know she'll find a way to blame me for him dying. Good grief: he was in Iraq! He's the one who joined the army, not me. He's the one who volunteered to go over there and train the locals on how to use the artillery. He's the one who got himself killed, not me! But it's going to be my fault and she's going to yell at me and ignore her granddaughter...or even worse, call her horrid names...and...and..."

Bea held her close. Evidently Kizzie didn't have a clue that Butch had killed himself. That he didn't die in warfare or in an accident. Since Heath hadn't clued her in, she'd do it herself. Pull that Band-Aid off quickly.

She bit her lip, thinking about it. She'd seen the way Heath looked at her when they first came in and it wasn't sympathy—he wanted to take care of her as his own. Even if Kizzie had never shown a romantic interest in Heath, Bea knew she liked and respected him as a person. It wasn't her job to explain that he'd died by his own hand, and certainly Heath planned to let her know eventually, but she'd take one for the team on this one, be the first one Kizzie lashed out at when she found out that Butch was a coward and took the easy way out.

"Kizzie, I'm not going to ask you if you're okay. I overheard you say something about that to Heath. What I'm going to tell you is going to make you mad or sad all over again. Shoot! It might even make you throw up, but I don't think you'll pass out. Are you ready for this?"

"No but tell me anyway."

"Kizzie, Butch killed himself. There was no accident. The report Heath got said his death was under investigation."

"Oh," Kizzie said without emotion, as if she'd just been given the answer to a math problem.

"Aren't you upset?" Bea asked.

"They're sure someone didn't murder him?"

"No! I mean, I don't know. I mean, if they suspected murder, there would have been mention of looking for the culprit or he or she was in custody."

"Do you know how he did it?" Kizzie asked indifferently.

"No. Does it matter?"

"No. I guess not." Kizzie paused as she thought, her lips working from a frown to a smile, ending in a chuckle.

"You know, this could have gone south in a hurry. I mean, I could be a total wreck with what you just told me, but in a way, it's a relief. First, I could have guilt because I sent him what some could have called a Dear John letter. But I never mailed it. It's still in the diaper bag. Second, it just shows what a chicken shit he was. He had something going on with all the money he took. Probably gambling, although when we got married, he promised he'd never do it again. He probably had other things going on that we agreed he'd quit, too."

Bea was stunned, her eyes wide in shock, but she remained still.

Kizzie laughed again, this time a nervous giggle. "Yeah, he had a string of girls on the side. He never did drugs, and said beer was his only vice. He said he used a condom so sex with them didn't count: they wouldn't get pregnant. Shoot! Maybe he got another gal pregnant and she had a less than ideal baby, too. Now that would really send him over the top."

"Kizzie, I think you're getting carried away. All we know officially is that his death is under investigation. Don't damn him anymore than he is already."

The nervous smirk turned into a frown. "Yeah, you're right. I'll just focus on the procedure. I think the pamphlet Heath gave me outlines who to contact about everything. Step one, step two..." She shook her head, thinking about how much crap she'd be going through in the next month.

"You know Zeke and I are here for you. And Heath, too. He's fond of you and wants to make sure you have all the assistance you need."

Kizzie's mouth twitched, trying to contain the smile at hearing Heath was fond of her. Her eyes brightened, remembering that he said he'd be out of the service soon. "I'll take all you three can give me. And hugs from Zoe, LuLu and the boys, too."

Chapter 8

"Hello. I'd like to speak to Mr. or Mrs. Wadsworth, please. This is Captain Heath King of the United States Army. This is official business."

"I'm sorry, sir. They're on holiday. They took a cruise to Alaska. They're supposed to be arriving in Anchorage this evening via the train they're catching from Seward. I can give you their cell phone numbers, if you'd like," the young woman said. "You did say this was regarding their son, right?"

"No, I said it was official business," Heath said, concerned that the woman was so free in giving out what he considered privileged information.

"Oh, I just thought that you were the one they'd contacted about getting their son out of Iraq. I guess they called in some favors from a senator or something, and Butch was supposed to be back in Anchorage at the same time they were going to show up. I just didn't want to spoil the surprise for him."

"Thank you very much. Let me confirm the phone numbers…"

The woman cut him off, quickly rattling off the numbers even though she still hadn't confirmed what the phone call was regarding. "Those are the numbers I have here, too. Thank you. If I need more information, may I get your name?"

"Oh, I'm Cynthia. I'm his fiancée. We're going to get married as soon as his divorce is final. I guess that's going to be pretty soon from what Mother Wadsworth tells me."

"All right. Thank you again."

"Right. See ya!"

Heath pushed end call and looked at his phone in shock. "Good grief! That guy was a major creep! Not even divorced and has a fiancée already? What was he thinking?"

Rather than dwell on the situation, real or feigned by a bubble-headed sprite, Heath opened his browser and searched William Wadsworth images, looking for pictures of the parents so he'd know who they were when he arrived at the train station.

And there they were, just as he imagined them after the personality profile Kizzie had shared. The perfectly coifed and designer-attired matron without an extra ounce of body fat and her slump-shouldered, mousy-mustached husband behind her left shoulder, offering her support if needed. *Or tapping into her spine for one of his own.*

No wonder Kizzie didn't want to tell them—not that it was her responsibility—but by their names, these were high society types, old money from early America. He didn't need to verify it. Their posture said more than four pages of results on an internet search engine.

He looked at his watch. Four hours until he needed to head to the railroad station. He'd let Bea tend to Kizzie and Zoe. Time to go home for a change of clothes, freshen up his uniform, and then a power nap. He'd need all the strength he could muster to face Mother Wadsworth.

***

Almost like a hologram of the image on the internet, the continental couple stepped lightly off the train onto the bright yellow step stool, Mrs. Wadsworth wearing gloves and a string of pearls, her wrist limp as she offered her hand to the conductor to assist her in stepping off. It was a wonderfully warm June evening—mid-70 degrees temperature—yet the grand dame was wearing a fur trimmed off-white cardigan, her ivory linen slacks as crisp as when they had come out of the closet.

Lord, give me strength! "Good evening and welcome to Anchorage. You are Mr. and Mrs. William Wadsworth, I presume."

"Mr. and Mrs. Wadsworth the second," she corrected. "And you are…"

"Sir, Madam, I am Captain Heath King of the United States Army. If you'll indulge me, I'd like to have a word with you in private."

Mrs. Wadsworth looked to her husband, a slight smile of victory on her face. "Yes, yes, let's get away from the crowds. First we were crammed into the ocean liner and then stuffed into the train." She lifted her chin and pointed with it toward the umbrella-shaded tables at the end of the depot. "How about some fresh air?"

Great. Far enough away that she can't throw too much of a fit, but close enough that I can still get them to the car and haul them away if they do make a big scene. Still with me, Lord?

"William, dust off the chairs for the Captain and me, if you would."

"Yes, dear," William said dryly, as if he was a robot and his programmer had forgotten to insert an emotion chip. He pulled a bar towel out of his hip-slung satchel and did a quick but efficient wipe down of the chairs and table top. He pulled out the chair for his wife, then cleaned off a chair for himself.

Heath thought about standing up to deliver the news but didn't want to be standing over them when he spoke. Besides, if she was already seated, she'd only slump forward and not hit the ground if she fainted.

"Madam, Sir, it is my sad duty to inform you that your son has died. He passed from this earth on June 25 while in Iraq. The circumstances of his death are currently under investigation."

First stage: shock.

Neither one of the Wadsworths spoke, Mr. Wadsworth even more pale than his wife. Then Heath realized that her makeup masked the blood draining from her face. She was probably even more shocked than her husband, but it didn't show through the layers of colored talc.

Second stage: denial

"No, no. You're mistaken, Captain King," Mrs. Wadsworth said. "He was an advisor, not active military. He didn't even carry a gun. He promised me he'd be safe. I even made arrangements for him to come home early. I sent him money to give the officer in charge as a bonus, so he'd be back in Alaska today. That's why we're here. He was supposed to pick us up from the train station, and then we could take him back with us to Connecticut. I figured he got delayed so he sent you to let us know where and when he'd meet us."

"No, ma'am. I'm sorry, ma'am. I received the official report this morning."

Third stage: anger

"You're wrong! This must be the ruse his commanding officer made up so he could sneak back in the states. I'm telling you, you'd better get your facts straight before you start upsetting family. I can have your job or commission or whatever it's called like this." She tried to snap her fingers, but her gloves made it impossible. "Show him, William," she said to her husband.

Mr. Wadsworth looked sideways at Heath, lost in grief and shock, then back at his wife. He did as he was told, lifting one hand to give a weak 'snap,' his strength sapped by the news that his son, his only child, was dead.

Fourth stage: Bargaining

"I'll tell you what," she said, her face leaned in toward Heath with an attitude of collusion. "You give me the name and number of his commanding officer in Iraq and I'll talk with him and find out what really happened. Butch told me that there might be complications, that he might have to, shall we say, stretch the truth a little. I'm sure that's what happened here. You help me out and I'll see if I can pull a few strings, so you can get an early release, too."

Heath looked at her husband to see if he had heard, and if so, what he thought. The gray-haired man was still glassy-eyed, wallowing in stage one shock, oblivious to his wife's attempt at controlling life.

"Ma'am, I'm sorry. He really did die. They're shipping his body here tomorrow. I'm not sure if it's going to be an open casket—that depends on what his wife decides—but I can schedule a viewing if it helps you get closure."

"Screw you! And screw her, too! If he really is dead, then it's all her fault. He only went over there because she wanted more money. He gives her half his allowance and it still isn't enough for her. I think she has a drug problem. Or maybe it's gambling. I can't remember. It's one of those, I'm sure. And you're letting her decide on the funeral? Why? I'm his mother!"

"She's his wife. 'For this reason, a man shall leave his

father and his mother, and be joined to his wife; and they shall become one flesh.'"

"Oh, don't go quoting that Bible nonsense to me. He's my son. If he really is dead, I'll make the funeral decisions!"

"I'll let her know that you asked to be in charge of the arrangements. Is there anything else I can help you with?"

She stood up and screeched, "What? Are you kidding me? You tell me my son is dead and that worthless lump of wife who screwed around on him and had a messed-up baby that she refused to get rid of is going to take care of his funeral arrangements! She's going to be richer than the Queen of Sheba with that life insurance policy she took out on him. That…that…"

"Martha, that's enough," William said, his hand on her elbow, urging her to calm down. "The captain already said he'd speak with…with…Oh, what is her name?"

"Kizzie," Heath said, his jaws clenched tight.

"Yes, thank you. The captain said he'd speak with Kizzie about letting you take charge of the funeral. I'll give him our phone numbers and he can let us know either way. Now, come on. Let's get a taxi and go to the hotel. It's been a long two weeks and I don't think my heart can take any more stress."

"Oh, you and your heart..." she said, dismissing his problems with a wave of her hand.

"I have your phone numbers," Heath said. "I ...ahem... verified them with Cynthia earlier today."

"Oh! Oh, my," William said. "I forgot about her. She's going to be heartbroken. But, she's young and she'll find another beau in no time. I assume the taxis are out front?"

"Yes, sir, but I can take you to wherever you need to go."

"No. Thank you," Mrs. Wadsworth said curtly. "Come on, William. I'll make a few calls and find out what's really going on. A funeral—pft!"

Mr. Wadsworth looked at Heath, his sorrow unmistakable. "Thank you for being gentle," he said. "She can be downright pigheaded sometimes. I assume I'll see you at the funeral?"

"Most likely," Heath said. "Peace be with you and yours in this time of sorrow."

"Thanks. I'll do my best."

"Are you going to stay chit chatting with that man or are we going to the hotel?"

He looked at Heath one more time, shrugged one shoulder, then walked toward his wife. "I'm coming, Martha.

I'll be right there."

***

"Hi, Zeke," Heath said. "Sorry to call so late. How's Kizzie doing?"

"She's doing better than I expected. Bea shared a few things with me, so under the circumstances, yes, she's doing fine. Of course, there's no way we're going to let her out of our sight for a month. At least!"

"I just told her husband's parents the news. The mother was in complete denial. She offered me a bribe to give her his commanding officer's phone number in Iraq so she could find out what really happened. I guess she sent over a large sum of money to buy him an early release. I'll do a little more research and call the chaplain there and see if he has any insight on Butch's character and any shady dealings he might have been involved with. How are my girls adjusting to their new room?"

As soon as the words were out of his mouth, Heath shut his eyes and groaned softly.

"*Your* girls? Are you taking responsibility for them already? The man's body hasn't even hit the States, much less been buried. You'd better slow down there, Heath. Not that I blame you. She's sweet on you, too. I don't know what you told her today, but when your name comes up, so do her ears and eyebrows. She looks like a cotton-pickin' rabbit checking the surroundings for her mate."

"Really?" Heath perked up, then blushed, glad that he was on the phone and couldn't be seen. "I'm sorry. I'm just tired. I tried to take a nap before going into Anchorage to meet his parents but that didn't work. I couldn't shut my brain off. I looked them up on the internet so I'd recognize them. Yup. They're old money but that doesn't mean their bucks are going to be around for long. There's a big lawsuit pending that's been ongoing for at least five years. They're probably going to have to sell everything and take up residency in the poorhouse pretty soon. Dollars to donuts Butch knew all about it. He was named in the lawsuit, too."

"You know, I pride myself with meeting just about everyone here on post, but I think I missed him."

"I guess he was pretty easy to spot: six-foot six-inches tall, good-looking…"

"Full of himself… Yeah, I met him. Or saw him leave. I asked what was going on and no one knew. He just got tired of my 'welcome to post' speech, I guess, and took off." Zeke shook his head. "How'd she ever wind up with a loser like that?"

"We all make mistakes," Heath said. "I'll be by in the morning. I want to talk to Kizzie face-to-face about something. Butch's mother wants to take care of the funeral arrangements even though she doesn't believe he's dead. She thinks it's part of his ruse to sneak home early. His poor dad is so hen-pecked, he doesn't have even a pin feather left. He believed me that Butch was dead, though, and seemed genuinely sad about it. I'll have to watch out for him, though. He mentioned something about having a bad heart. She poo-pooed it, but I get the feeling that if it isn't about her or her son, she doesn't care about it."

"Okay. I'll see you tomorrow morning. I won't be going in to work until later, so I'll have coffee waiting."

"All right. Too bad there's so much to do. I could really do with an hour or so of smacking the color off a few dozen golf balls."

"Me, too," Zeke said. "Me, too."

***

Knock. Knock.

"Come on in, Heath. Coffee, bacon, eggs, toast...or if you're really brave, I think I have some toaster pastries in the cabinet," Zeke said. "I was sorta waiting for you. Kizzie is sleeping in."

Heath stepped into the kitchen and saw Bea with a big breakfast spread in front of her, Zoe on her lap munching a triangle of toast.

"Hey, there, Heath. Come on over. I'm getting the queen for a day treatment. The boys and LuLu already ate. They're outside, chasing butterflies with the nets we made yesterday out of old nylons and wire coat hangers."

"Before Kizzie wakes up, I wanted to tell you what I found out last night. It may have been ten o'clock here, but it was nine in the morning in Iraq. I got more than I was looking for. Not only was Butch chin deep into gambling, he had set up an arms deal. The guy on the other end turned him in. Or was getting ready to. Nothing took place, but the buyer came on post, looking to sell information on the pending deal to the colonel, then found out that Butch had killed himself. I guess Butch never had anything to sell but was going to try to get the man's money, then concoct some story about why he couldn't deliver.

"When he found out he wasn't going to get a reward for that information, the buyer decided to spill more. He let the colonel know about the floating gambling game. I guess everyone who ever participated knew that hot-headed Butch couldn't lay off the long shots. Blackjack was his game of choice. Whether the dealer baited him with letting him win a few hands to get him in deep or not didn't make a difference. Gambling is *verboten*."

"So? That wasn't a reason to kill himself," Bea said.

"Well," Heath looked to make sure Zeke was listening, too. "I guess he'd been dipping into his family's living allotment to cover some of his gambling debts." He rolled his eyes at Bea. *I found this out from a different source, so I'm not compromising the secret you accidentally shared.* "That wasn't enough, so he sold his insurance policy, too. He even cashed in his living allotment and was staying in an old tent that had been scrapped. Not even a pot to piss in."

"Wow," Bea and Zeke said at the same time.

"And it gets worse. When I called his parent's house yesterday to tell them the bad news, a young woman answered. She said they were going to be arriving in

Anchorage in a few hours."

"So, when you spoke to them last night, you talked to them in person?" Bea asked.

"Yes. I guess I forgot to tell you about that," Heath said, trying to remember the conversation.

"You may have told Zeke, but I didn't know it. Go on."

"It gets worse. When I asked the young woman on the phone her name for my report, she told me it was Cynthia."

"Yeah. So?" Bea said.

"She said she was his fiancée."

"Oh, crap," Bea said, then turned to Zoe. "You don't need to learn that word, sweetie. How about, 'Oh, pooh!'"

Zeke brought his coffee mug to the table and sat down. "You mean to tell me that you met his parents in Anchorage last night, that his mother didn't believe you when you said he'd died, and that they knew he was engaged to be married? Did they think he was divorced?"

"Nope. Cynthia said as soon as the divorce was final, she and Butch were going to get married."

"Oh, cra... Oh, pooh!" Zeke said.

"Pooh!" Zoe cried out, all smiles at learning a new word.

"Well, I'm glad we cleaned up our language for this

103

conversation," Bea said. "How are we going to tell Kizzie?"

"You don't have to. I just heard the whole thing." Kizzie took her daughter from Bea and snuggled a kiss into her chest, eliciting a giggle from the baby. "And I agree. Oh, pooh."

"I'm so sorry," Heath said. "I just found out last night. I...I..."

"Don't worry about it. It actually should make my life easier. Folks feel sorry and extend sympathy to widows. Divorced women, especially those who divorced a husband who was deployed overseas at some point, are more likely to get scorned, shunned. Plus, there's the cost. No divorce lawyers, no property settlements and no custody battle—as if he ever wanted anything to do with my little angel. But you said he sold his life insurance policy? I guess I can't be any broker than I am now."

"Did you hear the part about his mother? She's in town and wants to take care of the funeral," Heath said, his arms aching to hold her and the baby close.

"Let her," she said, a chill running up her spine at the thought of her former mother-in-law, the Ice Queen. She turned toward Heath and suddenly felt warm and safe. She wanted to snuggle into his arms, ask him to hold her and never let go, but now was definitely not the time or place. She settled for sitting across from him at the table, accepting the cup of coffee Zeke handed her for the warmth she craved.

She took a sip of coffee and said to Heath, "I looked up the stages of grief you were talking about. I'm not sure, but I think I've made it to the testing stage: seeking realistic solutions. If I ever went through the previous step, depression, it was awfully short. Actually, I'm pretty sure I had the depression for a couple of years before he killed himself. It was a horrible feeling, but I don't have it anymore. I'm sure glad it's out of the way and I hope it never comes back."

"Yes, I think ceding the funeral to his mother is a realistic solution to dealing with his death, especially for her. She's still in denial. From what I can see, she'll be there until she sees his body. By the way, it's supposed to get here about noon. Did you want me to schedule a viewing for you?"

Kizzie pursed her lips and stifled the bad words that were trying to sneak out. Rather than try to find an inoffensive reason for why she didn't want anything else to do with

Butch—either dead or alive—she shook her head and uttered a quick but definite, "No."

Chapter 9

"This came for you in the mail, sir," the corporal said. "It was addressed to your house, but since you're seldom there and the letter carrier knew where you worked, she dropped it off to me. It was certified mail and needed a signature. I didn't think you'd mind."

"Thanks." Heath took the oversized envelope to his desk and was ready to open it when his cellphone rang. He looked at the caller ID, saw the out of state area code, then remembered it had to be either Butch's mother or father. "Captain Heath King. How may I help you sir or ma'am?"

"Captain King, this is Mrs. Wadsworth. We met last night at the train depot in Anchorage. I want you to know that I still don't believe you but am willing to go through the motions for the sake of propriety. Are you the person I contact about making...hee, hee...funeral arrangements?"

She's laughing? She still thinks this is part of some con Butch put together to get out of the service? She's in for a very rude awakening!

"Ma'am, you can meet the coroner this afternoon at two

o'clock. You and your husband can work out the details with him."

"My husband won't be joining me. I rented a car and will be there this afternoon. I know where the post is but what is the coroner's address?"

"Ma'am, you'll have to come to the post gate to check in, show your identification, then a soldier will come get you and escort you to the funeral home. You can't just come driving in. This is a restricted access facility."

"Well! I never! A woman loses her son, her only child, and the army doesn't show her any respect."

Your son was a lying, thieving coward who shot himself. We're showing him a lot more respect than he'd get in the outside world! "Ma'am, those are the rules for everyone. Shall I let them know you'll be coming in at two o'clock?"

"Yes, you might as well." Click.

Heath looked at the phone and shook his head in disbelief.

"Is everything all right, sir?"

"Yes and no. We'll know more this afternoon when she sees her son. I guess for her, seeing is believing." He chuckled and put the phone in his pocket. "Or maybe not with her. It's easy to see where Butch got his compulsion to play the long shots. She's doing the same thing by believing he's still alive." Heath picked up the pile of incoming reports, ready to immerse himself in anything but the Wadsworth family.

"Aren't you going to open the envelope, sir?" the corporal asked. "I know you have a lot on your mind, and it isn't any of my business, but it might be time sensitive."

"Oh, good grief. Thanks." Heath opened the envelope and saw it was the documents he had requested. Now that he had her birthdate and his DNA profile, a world of information about his sister was about to be available to him. All he had to do was search.

***

"Excuse me, sir," the corporal said. "Didn't you want to be at the mortuary when Mrs. Wadsworth was due in?"

Heath looked at his watch. Whoa! He'd been accessing data bases for four hours. Time flew when working on a project of love.

"Yes and no. No, I don't *want* to be there, but yes, I should be there. I want you to accompany me. It's time you got your feet wet. Or wetter. It was a bit intense with Kizzie. I'm glad you were with me."

"I can see why you need two people, sir, especially if there are young ones involved." The corporal grabbed his hat and took a deep breath. "I guess I'm as ready as I'll ever be. I've never seen a dead body up close. Scratch that. I've never seen a dead human body. Ever. Road kill moose don't count."

"Unless you're the one who hit it and you have to clean up the mess or get the car repaired afterwards. Let's hustle. I want to be there before she arrives."

***

"Good afternoon, Captain King, Corporal. Lieutenant Wadsworth's mother hasn't arrived yet. Everything is in place. Thanks for the warning about her not believing her son was dead. I've been doing this for fifteen years and, yes, it does happen on occasion, but usually it's when the body has only been identified by forensics."

Heath saw the look of confusion on the corporal's face and explained. "Captain Forsythe is talking about the cases where only a few remains are found, either because the person died in an explosion or fire, or they returned from a conflict that happened decades earlier in a foreign country." He looked up. "I think they're here now."

"Well, I never…" Mrs. Wadsworth huffed as the sergeant held the door open for her.

The soldiers looked at each other, wondering what had happened, but nothing was obvious.

"You can't carry a gun on post, ma'am, even if you have a concealed weapons permit. You'll get it back when you leave," the sergeant said, exasperated, as if this was the sixth time he had explained it to her.

"Mrs. Wadsworth, let me extend my deepest condolences," Captain Forsythe said and offered his hand.

"Yeah, yeah," she said and brushed it away. "Where are the caskets and such? I need to pick out the nicest one for my son."

"That's already been arranged, ma'am. In the forms he filled out when he enlisted, he stipulated that he wanted to be cremated. I thought you were here to bring us photos you'd like to share at the services and to say good-bye to him," Forsythe said, then looked to Heath. *You were right. She's totally in denial.*

"Cremated? Pshaw! I'm his mother and I'll decide what's

best for him. Now, let me see the caskets or brochures or whatever it is you have. And flowers. Do I pick out the arrangements here or do I have to go to the florist shop? Is there one nearby?"

"Ma'am, your son's express wish was to be cremated. You can't override that, and he can't change his mind now that he's…gone," Heath said. "I think you need to come in back with me and Captain Forsythe."

Heath put his hand near her elbow but knew the excitable woman wouldn't want him to touch her.

She glared at him, daring him to proceed, then blew out a breath of exasperation. "If viewing the body will stop all this nonsense, I'll do it. I'm telling you right now, though, he arranged with his commander in Iraq to get out early. This is all for show. He's probably on his way back to Connecticut right now. I'm sure it's some other poor unfortunate soul you have in the chiller." She shuddered at her words. "Come on. I guess I'm as ready as I'll ever be."

Captain Forsythe led the way, Heath and the corporal following behind the belligerent woman.

"I guess it's chilly in here for a reason," she said, and added a nervous giggle. "Well, get on with it!"

She folded her arms across her sweatered chest and tucked her hands under her armpits, trying to get them warm.

Forsythe pulled the sheet back, exposing the head and shoulders of the corpse, the cloth bandage disguising the fact that the back of the soldier's skull had been blasted away by his 9 mm service revolver.

Heath and the corporal were at her heels, ready to catch her when she passed out, but they weren't needed. She did grasp the edge of the table, though, her knees buckling briefly.

"He did such a good job of finding a doppelganger. This man looks so much like my Butch."

"Ma'am," Forsythe said, "they matched the fingerprints, too. This is your son."

"Hmph! If it was my son, he'd have six toes on his right foot. I seriously doubt any body double would be able to duplicate that!"

She stepped to the end of the table and grasped the end of the sheet.

Heath and the corporal rushed to either side of her.

She pulled the shroud off dramatically, took one look, then said, "Oh, shit!" and fainted.

"Some people just won't believe what you say, no matter what," the corporal said. "Now what'll we do?"

"I have smelling salts right here," Forsythe said, patting his chest pocket. "Do you want to give her a minute?"

Heath looked side to side, lips pursed in frustration, hoping for inspiration. "Yes, wait a minute. Cover him up again, then let's get her out of here before we rouse her. I don't want her fainting all over again."

***

"Ma'am. Ma'am," Forsythe said, wafting the ammonia-filled snifter under her nose. "You have to wake up now."

Her eyes fluttered, then popped open and shut again, squeezed tight against reality.

"Mrs. Wadsworth," Heath said, his voice stern and uncompromising. "You have to get up. We'll have a driver take you to your hotel. I just talked to your husband. He's expecting you."

The woman was feigning unconsciousness, her eyes and lips wrinkled as she forced them closed.

"Well, then, I guess I'll just have to take you to the post medical center. Or would you rather go to the hospital in

Anchorage?"

Still no reply.

"All right, then," Heath said. "Post medical center it is. They don't have any private rooms, and you'll probably have to wait in the lobby for a couple hours before the medic can see you. Still, it's clean and better than spending the rest of the afternoon in a mortuary. Come on, Corporal—you grab her legs and I'll get her shoulders."

"Don't you dare!" she screeched, sitting up like someone had poured ice water on her head.

"Sorry about that, ma'am," Heath said. "I couldn't let you stay lying out here. And I truly am sorry for your loss..."

"Oh, shut up. It's all her fault, anyway. She should be arrested for murder. Or collusion or accessory or whatever it's called."

"Ma'am, I understand you're upset, but understand this, Kiz..., I mean, the Mrs. Wadsworth who was his wife had absolutely nothing to do with his death." Heath gritted his teeth, wishing he had let her feign unconsciousness and stay on the cold linoleum floor until she decided to get up and start moving by herself. It would have served her right to suffer a little chill-induced rheumatism.

"Corporal, would you make arrangements to take Mrs. Wadsworth to Anchorage? I…"

"No. I'll go by myself, thank you very much!" she snapped. "I've been enough inconvenience to you." She picked up her purse from the desk top where Captain Forsythe had set it, sniffed with resolve, then approached the door Heath held open for her, trying to make a composed and refined exit despite the runny nose and tears seeping out the sides of her heavily mascara-coated eyes.

"And with that," Heath said as he watched her pull on the rental car door handle the wrong way twice, "I'd say she has a cup of anger mixed with a pint or two of depression…and a lot more on the way."

"Are you sure she should drive, sir?" Corporal asked.

"Oh, I'm pretty sure she shouldn't, but there's no way I could stop her, so I didn't even try. She'd call a raven white with a dirty smudge if it suited her way of thinking. She's not all there now, but I bet she's been a quart short on common sense her whole life." Heath laughed at his own remark. "But I'm not taking odds on that. I gave up gambling in the second grade when I couldn't win at tic tac toe!"

"So, is there going to be a service?" the corporal asked.

"I'll give her a day or two to get back with us before we do anything more than turn him over for cremation. Those were his wishes, not hers, and I want to make sure they're honored." *Even if he wasn't an honorable person.*

"How about his wife? Shouldn't we ask her?"

"His widow," Heath corrected. "I'll go over there later and ask. I…um…don't think we'll both need to go if you want to get back to your family. I think she's progressed beyond the fainting stage."

The corporal smiled and nodded, his eyes saying, 'Smitten!' but not a sound uttered.

Heath saw the look and said, "The major's wife is there with her, so we'll be chaperoned if that's what you're thinking."

"No, sir. I wasn't thinking that at all," he replied, chewing back his smile. "If there isn't anything else, sir, I'll get back with Captain Forsythe and let him know that he's to proceed. The services will be put on hold until further notice."

Heath glanced over at his desk and remembered what he had been doing before they left. "Yes, go ahead and do that. I have a few other matters to attend to." He sat down at his computer, entered his password, and scanned through his email.

Voila!

'Congratulations! We have a very close match to your DNA profile. Please log into your account to see possible relatives.'

"I'll be right back, Corporal," Heath said. "I never took lunch, so I'm taking it now."

"Sir. Yes, sir," he replied, then said under his breath, "smitten."

Heath walked around back of the office building to the picnic area, the unofficial summertime lunch room. He could justify researching the Wadsworth controversy during business hours—and how could someone as spotty as Butch ever get to become an officer, even if he had a college degree—but this was family-related. His family.

Why hadn't he thought of it before? A simple DNA test, a measly hundred bucks, might lead to someone on either side of his family who might know what happened to his sister, which 'hospital' his parents had taken her to.

And there it was. The close relative 'could' be an aunt according to the results. He looked at the name. Annette Simpson. Neither first nor last name rang a bell. Of course, he never knew his mother's maiden name or much about her family. All he remembered was an Aunt Nettie who came to visit on holidays. She stopped coming about the time Willa was given to the hospital. When he asked where Aunt Nettie was the Christmas after Willa was gone, his father told him not to mention her name ever again, especially in front of his mother.

"Nettie..." Heath said, then laughed. "Annette is Nettie! If nothing else, I've found my Aunt Nettie. Maybe she'll know what happened to Willa."

Heath clicked on the contact form and sent a short email to her. 'I think I'm your nephew, Heath King. Would you please contact me and verify?' and signed his name and email. "Help me, Lord, on this. I really, really want to find my sister. I want just one more hug and to tell her she isn't—and never was—broken."

"Sir," the corporal called out, interrupting the soft-spoken prayer. "I think you'll want to take this call. It's William Wadsworth, the father."

"Thanks. I'll be right there." Heath put away his phone, took two deep breaths, and went back to work. He'd have to wait until later to share the good news with Bea and celebrate his discovery.

"Captain King speaking," Heath said, answering the phone in his office. "Yes, sir, I'd be happy to set up a meeting. I'll call you back at this number shortly. Thank you for reaching out."

Heath hung up the phone and looked at the corporal. "Well, I'll be. Butch's dad wants to see his granddaughter. And Kizzie. I'm not sure why, but it didn't sound like he was going to cuss them out or ask for money. I guess I'll see if she's interested."

***

"Come on, Zoe," Kizzie said as she set her daughter's feet on the floor inside the fast food restaurant. "Take a few more steps to Mama."

Zoe wavered slightly, finding her balance, then leaned forward and toddled four steps into her mother's arms.

Heath stood just outside the door, looking through the window at the two of them. "There they are, sir. Your daughter-in-law and granddaughter. Kizzie and Zoe."

"She's no longer our daughter-in-law," Mrs. Wadsworth snapped.

"Can it, Martha," William said, then pulled open the door. He looked back at his wife. "And be civil. Or just keep quiet. One or the other. Or both."

"Is that my little Zoe," he said, and sat in the chair next to Kizzie. "I'm your grandpa, Zoe. Your papa."

"Do you want to hold her?" Kizzie asked, turning the baby around so she could see him.

"Oh, I'd love to!" He took her and held her under her arms, letting her step on his slacks, bouncing her slightly as she tested her legs. "Can you say 'Papa'?"

"Papa," she said, then reached out and grabbed the end of his nose.

"Wow! She said a new word, Heath!" Kizzie said, then stood up next to him, stifling the urge to snuggle into his arms.

Grandpa turned his face slightly sideways, so she'd let go of his nose. "You are so precious, Zoe. I'm sorry I missed the first two years of your life, but if your mama will let me, I'll be here for you as long as my old ticker ticks."

Kizzie looked up at Heath and smiled, glad that she had someone to share the moment with. "Sounds good to me," she replied.

"Hmph!" Mrs. Wadsworth snorted.

"Mar-thaaa…" William warned with his tone.

She turned away from the display of happiness and discovery and went into the ladies room to sulk in solitude. *How'd Butch ever find a twin with the same six toes on the right foot? There must have been some surgery involved somewhere. He's probably in Connecticut right now, waiting for me, laying low so they don't know he fooled them. Yeah, that's right. He can't tell them he's alive—it'd spoil everything. I'll just play along for a while until I get home.*

"Kizzie, I'm sorry my family was so horrible to you. You didn't deserve it," William said. "Butch and his mother are two of a kind. I…I…"

She put her hand on top of his as he supported Zoe on his lap. "It's okay, Papa," she said, winking at his new name, "We forgive you. Or I forgive you. Zoe never knew the difference."

"Thanks," he said. "I needed that. The heart doctor said to keep away from stress, to take a cruise. Boy, was he wrong. Being cooped up with that woman," he nodded to the ladies room. "I'm sorry for all the conniving Butch did, trying to scam your father out of his legacy to you…"

"I sort of wondered about that," Kizzie said, "but I thought that when he found out I wasn't going to be an heiress and still married me, that he really did love me."

Papa shrugged one shoulder. "Maybe he thought your dad would change his will. He was playing the long shot, I suppose. Just like his mother. You know, she's probably going to wind up in prison for fraud. She and Butch wiped out his trust funds years ago. Enlisting as an officer was his last-ditch effort to achieve a respectable social standing.

"We're busted. Flat broke. We maxed out the charge cards and credit lines coming up here to Alaska. I'm surprised she had enough on a card to rent a car! They don't have anything on me. She wanted everything in his and her name so the two of them would get all the bucks." He chuckled. "Greed's a bitch."

He snuggled his face into Zoe's belly, then his tone softened again. "At least I got *some* good out of the boy. You're sure a cutie. Your eyes are the same deep green color as mine. And nobody'd better say anything bad about my girl. Ever."

William looked at Kizzie after his declaration of devotion to his granddaughter to see how she had taken it. Her face was streaming with happy tears, a sniffle now and then, but without words, overcome with joy that her daughter now had a grandparent. He looked up at Heath. "Thank you, too, Captain King, for setting this up."

"The name's Heath. And it's been my privilege, sir."

Heath looked towards the tap-tap-tap noise coming from the counter area. Martha Wadsworth had left the concrete cave of isolation and reflection—the restroom—and was standing near the registers, letting her presence be known. She looked at her watch, still tapping her toe. "Our flight takes off in four hours and we still have to get the rental car back. I'm hungry, but I certainly don't want to eat this garbage. There's bound to be a five-star restaurant somewhere in downtown Anchorage."

William looked to Heath, then Kizzie, and sighed in defeat. He gave Zoe another big hug. "Can you say good-bye to Papa?" he asked and took her hand and waved it. He let go of it, and she continued to wave. "Papa, Papa," she said.

"My life is complete. I could die tomorrow and be a happy man."

Kizzie stood up and hugged him around his shoulders. "Don't do that. Every little girl needs a grandpa." She looked toward his impatient wife. "And if she's going up river, you can spend more time with us."

William's eyes sparkled. "Now that's a happy thought that'll get me through lots of her yabbering. That and these," he pulled a piece of plastic out of one ear. "She thinks their hearing aids, but they're really ear plugs." He laughed and replaced it. "You still have my number." He turned to Heath. "And you do, too. Make sure she's okay for me, Heath. If she needs anything…" He shrugged a shoulder. "I can't give her money, but I can give her and my little Zoe lots of love. Bless you all."

"Are you about finished there?" Mrs. Wadsworth shouted across the dining area.

"Put a cork in it, Martha. I told you to be civil or be quiet. We'll leave when I'm ready." He looked at his watch, eyes wide at the time, and said, "And I'm ready."

"Have a safe—and peaceful—flight," Heath said, winking at the word peaceful, and waved good-bye to the pair, glad that one of them was gone.

"Are you two okay here? I'd offer to take you back to Bea's, but I don't have a car seat for Zoe."

"No, we're fine. Actually, I'm more content than I've been

in years. It's so nice to see that William cut the puppet strings held by his wife. She doesn't have anything to yank on anymore. I really do hope he can spend the rest of his life in peace."

"Me, too. I have a few more things to finish, and then I'll pop by to see how my girls are doing when I'm done."

"Don't take too long. I'm sorta getting used to having you around. I miss you when you're gone. Oh, I'm not supposed to talk like that, am I? Aren't I supposed to be in mourning?"

"Kizzie, from what you've told me, you've been in mourning for the last two years."

"At least." Kizzie stood up and offered him Zoe, an excuse to stand close to him.

Heath took the little girl in his arms, then gave her a squeeze and a kiss on the top of her blonde hair. "I'll drop by Bea's when I'm done. I think I might have some good news to share." He handed Zoe back to Kizzie, wishing he could hug her, too. *Maybe sooner than later if she really does feel as if she's been in mourning for two years!*

***

Heath waited until he had pulled up in front of his office

before he opened his email to see if he had a reply from Aunt Nettie yet. "Hoo! Hoo!" he said and pumped his fist in the air.

My dear sweet nephew,

It was so good to hear from you. With all the relocations your father went through, I lost track of where you were. Do you have any idea how many Kings there are in the US Army? After your father died, there was no way I could track you down. Occasionally, I search the internet for you, but I forgot your real name was Heath. Your parents always called you Bubba when you were little, at least while I was still in your life.

If you ever get a chance to come down to McMinnville, Oregon, please drop in and see us anytime. We have lots to catch up on and I'd rather do it face-to-face.

Love,

Aunt Nettie

"Oh, I am so taking a long weekend off! Family emergency time, here I come."

Dear Aunt Nettie,

Is day after tomorrow too soon?

Heath 'Bubba' King

Heath went back to work, too excited to concentrate on

the pile of folders on his desk. "All right, here I go…" While the corporal was out of the office, Heath made a few phone calls. He had less than two weeks left of his commission, but this was urgent. He checked his email for the tenth time in the last half hour and there it was. *'Come on down! Let me know what time you'll be here and if you need a ride. Here's a map link to our location and my phone number. Love, Aunt Nettie*

The clerk on the phone said, "Don't forget, sir, you'll have to have Major Zaharis sign off on the leave. It usually takes weeks to get time off, if that. He has quite a few requests ahead of yours."

"Yes, but this is an emergency and he's fair," Heath said. "Fax me the papers and I'll take care of getting the signature."

"You look a little flushed, sir," the corporal said when he came back from his errand. "Is there something wrong?"

"No, no. All's fine, however I'll have to ask you to take over everything for a few days. I'm going to fly down to the Lower 48 the day after tomorrow and won't be back for four days. I'm sure you can handle everything here."

Heath shuffled through the folders on his desk, too excited

to focus. "On second thought, maybe I can fly out tonight."

"I don't think you're going to be worth a darn here, so you might as well be wherever it is you're going. I've never seen you so flustered."

Beep!

Heath heard the fax machine notification then rushed over and grabbed the papers from it. "You're right—I think I'll see what I can do. I'm done for the day. I'll see you tomorrow. Or not, depending on whether I'm here or not."

"Good afternoon, Captain King," Zeke said as he walked in the front door. "I was wondering if you were free this evening. I have a bucket of red golf balls that need the color knocked off of 'em," he said with a wink.

"Oh, Major Zaharis. I was just coming your way for a signature. Something's come up with family and I need to take a few days emergency leave."

Zeke scowled, then put his hand on Heath's shoulder. "Walk with me a moment."

Heath led the way out of the office to the picnic area. "Heath, I didn't think you had any family left, other than that sister you and Bea have been searching for. Did you find her?"

"No, but I did find my mother's sister—just today. She's in McMinnville, Oregon. We've been back and forth via email and she said she has something to talk to me about, face-to-face. I need to go down there and check it out."

Zeke walked around the bench, his hands clutched behind his back. "You're sure this is legitimate and not some scam?"

"This all started with the DNA test I had done. Sir, I've never asked for time off for anything. I know this is a rough time with a new casualty, but my corporal has everything under control."

"And by everything, you mean Kizzie?"

"Yes, sir. She's attained closure. Actually, she reconnected with Zoe's grandfather—Butch's father—earlier today. He's head over heels for Zoe and wants to be a part of her world. Life is looking up for Kizzie now. She and Bea seem to be comforting each other, and sir, I've been waiting for this for as long as I can remember."

"Give me the papers and I'll sign them. Take as long as you need. I'll make sure 'your girls' are fine…"

Heath blushed, twice if that was possible—once for being called out for having a crush on the young widow and once for his commanding officer knowing about it. "I haven't talked to Kizzie about this yet. I just got the word. If I can't fly standby, I have lots of frequent flyer miles to use. Thank you, sir."

"I'll expect a full report when you get back, Captain. About the family issue, I mean. I can find out about Butch and the drama queen from Corporal Lent." Zeke didn't even try to stifle the chuckle that always came with saying the name. "Corpulent. Fat. Corporal Lent is anything but fat. I'm going to have to get him interested in officer training school, although Lieutenant Lent isn't too much better. Now, get crackin' with reconnecting with your family!"

"Sir. Yes, sir," Heath said, saluted and winked. "I'm on it!"

Chapter 10

Heath drove up to his house, hit the garage door opener in the console, and drove in. It wouldn't take long to throw a few items in his duffle bag but explaining what was going on to Kizzie and saying good-bye to her might take longer. His ride would arrive in ten minutes, but he should be able to make it. He opened the door from the garage into the house, intent on what to say…

"Hi."

"Yikes!" Heath squeaked and stepped back against the kitchen wall, breathless from the shock.

"I didn't mean to scare you," Kizzie said, her face pink in embarrassment. "I didn't break in, though." She held up the spare key on the lucky tee keychain he had given Zeke and Bea. "Bea had her phone on speakerphone when Zeke called to check in. I was there in the dining room with her and heard that you had to leave in a hurry to take care of a family issue. I'm sorry, but I never even thought about you having a family. I mean…"

Heath walked up to her and put his finger on her lip. "No

explanation needed. For the record, as far as I knew, all my family was gone. My mother and her sister had some disagreement years ago, so my aunt was out of my life. I never knew her last name or where she lived. And my only sibling…"

He dropped his hand and shrugged his shoulder, his eyes misting as he remembered his impassioned plea, *"Don't send her away—she's not broken!"*

"Look at me, Heath," Kizzie said. She reached up and put her hands in the crook between his neck and shoulders. "I mean *really* look at me."

A smile bloomed on his face as he did as she asked. *I'm looking into my future, right?*

Her lips met his, pensive at first, then hungry with desire. Her arms now wrapped around his neck, he lifted her off the ground. She wrapped both legs around his hips as he backed up towards the counter and spun around so she was pressed against it. Hands grabbed and tongues sought as they enveloped each other's bodies and emotions as far as they could within the restraints of clothing and counters.

She pulled back for a deep breath of air, then slid her lips down his five o'clock-shadowed neck. "I'm going to get whisker-burns if I'm not careful," she mumbled as she moved her mouth across his flesh, inhaling his scent, memorizing it.

Buzz! Buzz! Buzz!

"What's that?" she asked, then went back to skimming his skin with her lips, moving higher, exploring more of his body.

"Nothing," he said, fighting the urge to take her to his bedroom.

Buzz! Buzz! Buzz!

"It's not nothing," she whispered near his ear. "It's distracting."

"Oh, shi… Pooh!" Heath pulled away slightly, took his phone out of his pocket, and groaned as he saw an Oregon area code on the missed call.

"Not that I wasn't thoroughly enjoying myself," Kizzie said, "but I think you'd better call that number back. Family, right? Don't worry. I'm not going anywhere. I mean, you don't want me to, do you?"

"No! I mean, I'll have to leave for a few days, but I really, really want you in my life." He saw the precocious smile on her face. "You little minx. You were testing me, weren't you?"

"I don't think it was so much a test as a single question. I was pretty sure I felt that special vibe from you, and I already knew how I felt. I just wanted to confirm." She wiggled her hips next to the fly of his pants. "Now I know it's not just sympathy that has you looking at me the way you do."

Buzz! Buzz! Buzz!

"Take the call! We'll talk later," Kizzie said, then moved away to give him space. And to compose herself.

What were you thinking, throwing yourself at him like that? You know he's a chaplain and has a higher standard to live up to. Yeah, well he's still a man. And he's definitely interested—both his brain and his body.

"I'd say, 'Where were we?'" Heath said, breaking her reverie with a kiss on the top of her head, "but I don't think we'd better start again. I don't know if I could stop. It's not right. I mean, it's right, but it's too soon. I'm taking the next flight to Seattle, then driving to McMinnville. That's where she lives in Oregon. Right now, my life has more questions than answers."

Heath bent down and kissed her upturned face gently, slowly, savoring the peace she shared, the promise of a future together. He pulled back. "But you're the answer to probably the biggest question in this man's life: will I ever find the one?"

Kizzie tip-toed up and wrapped her arms around his neck. "It's amazing—we both had the same question and found our answer at the same time and place, right here. Together." She let go and patted his shoulders in dismissal. "Now, get going so you can get back. Don't forget to call Bea with the news. She said she'd let you tell me what this is all about."

Heath looked at his watch. "My ride is going to be here in about two minutes. Let me pack and then we'll talk."

Honk! Honk!

"Go grab your goodies," Kizzie giggled, "I mean gear, and I'll tell him you're on your way."

"I promise you'll be able to grab my goodies at some point," he called back from the bedroom, "But let's do it when we have more than a few seconds."

"Sir. Yes, sir," Kizzie said, then saluted with a bright smile.

He came out of the bedroom, duffle slung over his shoulder, and popped a quick kiss on her lips. "Take care of everything while I'm gone. I...I adore you, Kizzie."

"I adore you, too," she replied, and winked at him. She knew what he meant, and he knew that she knew.

"Ain't adore grand," she said softly as she watched him climb in the shuttle for the airport.

Heath pulled into the rest area and climbed into the back seat of the rental car. The flight had been nearly three and a half hours long, but that didn't mean he got that much sleep. Between the man next to him twisting and turning in his seat and the woman on the other side of him who had doused herself in cologne before she boarded, he was barely able to get a ten-minute nap. He set his duffle sideways in the back seat and positioned it under his neck... And he was out.

Three hours later, a trucker's horn blasted, it's brakes screeching to a halt a few feet from the car. Totally disoriented about where he was, what he was hearing, and what was lighting up the inside of the car, he sat up and looked behind him.

A big sixteen-wheeler semi had come to a stop a scant three feet from his rear bumper, the glare of the headlights temporarily blinding him.

The trucker climbed down from his tall cab. "I'm sorry," he said. "I thought this was the big rig side. Are you all right?" He noticed the uniform. "I mean, are you all right, sir?"

Heath chuckled at the man's unease, said, "Yes, I'm fine.

As you were."

"Okay. I was afraid I gave you a heart attack. I know that's what would have happened to me. Sir."

Heath grinned weakly, looked at his watch—3:30—and decided he might as well start his five-hour drive south.

One gas station and three coffee drive-through brews later, the sign said McMinnville 23 miles. He looked down at his hands. Shaking like he had the DTs. "Haste makes waste. Eat something so you don't rattle to pieces. Or pass out. That'd make a real good impression," he mumbled wryly.

After a quick egg sandwich and a freshen up with a change of clothes in the fast food restaurant bathroom, he decided he was ready. He rubbed the slight scruff on his neck, recalling the feel of Kizzie's mouth as she explored and enjoyed his exposed skin. *Not now. You can think of Kizzie and your future later. Now it's time to explore the past. Maybe, just maybe, she'll know where Mom and Dad took Willa. If she's still in the area, she shouldn't be too hard to find. Please, make it right, Lord.*

Heath pulled up to the older house at the edge of town. The white shiplap siding was peeling, but the yard was well-groomed, a diverse mixture of trees, shrubs, and flower beds spreading for nearly an acre around it, it's aroma clean yet sensual, a mixture of florals and spices.

"Here goes," he said and knocked on the door.

"Bubba? I mean, Heath?" the tall gray-haired woman asked. "Oh, my. You have to be with that straight posture and those broad shoulders. I'm your Aunt Nettie."

Another gray-haired woman walked into the room, drying her hands on a dish towel. "And this is your other aunt, my wife, Aunt Ellie."

Heath's eyes widened at the shock, but Aunt Nettie had expected it and waited for the fact that his aunt had a same-sex partner to set in before she started to talk again.

"We've had this place for almost twenty years now. We got it just after, shall we say, your mother and I had those final, caustic words. She didn't care for Ellie nor the fact that we wanted to spend the rest of our lives together." Nettie shook her head. "She always said there had to be something wrong with me—that I was broken—and that counseling and medications would fix me. As if!"

Heath didn't know what to say. Instead of trying to find the right words, he gave his aunt a big hug, then opened out one arm and looked to Ellie, asking her to join them with his smile.

"Neither one of you look broke to me," he said as he squeezed them close. "I'm glad I have family again."

He let them go, then sat down on the overstuffed floral-patterned sofa. "Aunt Nettie, I haven't led you on, but I have to tell you the whole truth. I wasn't looking for you when I found you. Don't get me wrong—it was a happy accident. I found you while I was looking for my sister. I've been looking for her since I was in high school. I know you remember Willa. Mother used to say she was broken, too." He shook his head, the fatigue of an intense few days wearing down his resolve to keep the tears of disappointment from leaking out.

"But she wasn't broken," he said, the tears beginning. "She was special. Different than everyone else. She shouldn't have given her away. I don't know if you know it or not, but I even tried to run away with her. Dad caught me, though. There was yelling and crying and…"

Heath broke down completely, Aunt Nettie holding him close, allowing him the tears he'd held back for so many years.

"Mama, is he okay?" a young woman asked.

"Yes, he's fine," Nettie said, then added, "Willa."

Chapter 11

Heath pulled away from his aunt and sat up straight. *I must be hearing things.* He wiped his eyes. "What did you say?"

"Hmm," she mused with a twinkle of mischief in her smile. She added softly, "I guess my daughter—your cousin—is related twice to you since she was born as your sister."

She turned to the petite woman standing in the doorway, a basket of rose blossoms in her arms and called out, "Willa, come say hi to Heath. He's come all the way from Alaska to see us."

Willa set the flowers down on the table in the dining room and extended her hand. "It's a pleasure to meet you, Heath."

Heath took her hand, his head moved back and forth in astonishment. "You, too," he said, mesmerized by seeing his once tiny baby sister as an adult woman. "You're so beautiful..." He pulled his hand back, shaking his head, trying to rattle some courtesy and respect into in. "I'm sorry. I mean, yes, you're a very sharp looking young woman, but I just spent a long time on the road after an overnight flight, after working all day, and… My goodness, you're so beautiful."

"Are you sure he's all right, Mama?" Willa asked.

"Sweetheart, remember when I told you I whisked you away when you were a baby because you were a princess growing up with the wrong parents?"

"Uh, huh…"

"And that there was a prince who I couldn't take with me at the same time? I wanted to, but the mother and father would only let me take one."

"And so my bubba had to stay with them and maybe one day, we could find him… Oh!" Willa turned to Heath. "Are you my bubba?"

Heath's tears started all over again. "Yes, I'm Bubba, your brother. I've been looking for you for…for years. I'm so glad your moms took good care of you. I wanted to, but I was only five and you were so tiny…" He grabbed a fistful of tissues from the box Ellie offered him. "Can I give you a hug?"

Willa looked to Nettie, then Ellie to make sure it was all right. "Yes, and I can hug you, too, Bubba."

Heath held her close and gave her a quick squeeze—at first, resisting the urge to rock her back and forth as he did when she was tiny and colicky—then gave in and tipped her sideways a couple of times before setting her back upright.

"Did you ever have hair?" she asked, staring at his close-cropped head.

"I still have hair, but I'm in the army. They'd rather I kept it short. My commission—that is, my job—is almost up with them. I was thinking of moving somewhere else, maybe someplace where I can have a garden. Is Oregon a nice place to live?"

"Why don't you show him *your* garden, Willa?" Nettie said. "I'll set out a little sampler while you're outside with him, let him know what we do around here."

Willa took his hand. "Come on, Bubba. Mama says I grow the biggest, most fragrant roses because I sing to them. I think maybe it's because I plant garlic next to them. They want to out-stink them so that's why they're more fragrant."

Heath toured the two-acre property with Willa. She knew the common name of every plant and the fancy Latin botanical names on a few of them. "We have over two hundred kinds of flowers and herbs here and that's not including the fifteen different kinds of fruit trees and," she rolled her eyes in exasperation, "berries. We have blackberries and blueberries and strawberries and loganberries and raspberries and marionberries and…" She looked to Heath to see if he needed her to continue her lengthy listing of berries.

"Wow! I get the idea. What do you do with all of them?"

"Well, we make jams out of the berries, teas out of some of the flowers and leaves, and scented lotions and shampoos and bath bombs and…"

There was that look again. The 'Do I have to keep up the list of items or do you understand?'

"I get the idea. You and your mothers have a little cottage industry going."

Willa squinted, looking at the house as if it was a mystery. "No, it's our home, a big house with a real big kitchen. A cottage is real small. Or at least smaller like that one," pointing to the smaller house at the other end of the gardens.

"Cottage industry is also a phrase," Heath said, and put his hand on her shoulder in reassurance. "How about if we go inside? I'm not used to the heat and I could use a drink of water."

It took a moment for Heath's eyes to adjust from the sunshine to the light indoors but when they did, he saw the spread Nettie had set out on the dining room table.

"Wow! Did you make all this?"

"Yup. The three of us along with the help of some of our friends. We have a little co-op going in the area. Some of the ladies from the group home a few miles up the road come over a few days a week and help us in the garden and also help process the fruits and flowers into the end products. A few weeks after harvest and processing, it's time for the big orders to start coming in. I have an online store and folks do their Christmas shopping while in their jammies. It pays the bills and then some. Shoot! I finally have money for a vacation but can't figure out how to get away for even two weeks. Ellie and I will be celebrating our twentieth anniversary in October. I'd love to take our motor home for a tour of the autumn leaves from here up to Canada. We have our passports—we just need someone to take care of Willa and the business while we're gone."

Heath shook his head in awe. Six months ago, he was a lonely chaplain, doing his best to save souls and comfort the lost. For weeks he'd been praying about what to do with his life. Earlier this week, he found his answer about 'who' he wanted in his life, and just now, he'd found his little sister, the subject of his obsessive lifetime search. And he also found his aunt—his kin who needed his help.

"How soon do you need me, and do you ever hold wedding ceremonies in the garden?" he asked, sporting the same mischievous smile his aunt flashed at him less than an hour earlier.

***

"Bea, are you sure he wouldn't mind?" Kizzie asked. "I tried to call him, but it went right to voice mail."

"Yes, I'm sure he wouldn't mind. Now, you need to get some rest. Zoe will be fine in that bed by herself. I'm up using the bathroom every two hours anyhow, so I'll check on her. Go ahead and stay at his place. Zeke said he asked for four days leave. I *thought* he'd have called me by now, but if he found what he was looking for, he's probably so wound up that he forgot."

"I'm really glad you're respecting his wishes with not telling anyone what he's up to. I mean, I know now that if I had a secret, you'd keep it, no matter what."

Bea smiled and asked, "So what secret are you burning to tell me? That you're in love with Heath and ready to run off with him? That he'd make the most perfect father for Zoe and never in your wildest dreams did you think the two of you would ever get so lucky as to find each other?"

Kizzie paled as her friend rattled off her innermost thoughts, as if Bea had sneaked into her heart and read her secret hopes and desires. She took a deep breath and swallowed, composing herself as best she could. "Close. Very close, except I don't believe in luck. I think I got blessed with him, especially considering he's a chaplain. I don't think preachers believe in luck, either."

"Well, you take tonight to sleep on it. Reflect on where you want to go with him. You need to recharge your batteries and sleeping with a toddler in a single-sized bed isn't doing it. Get some real rest. I'll see you in the morning for breakfast. Or lunch. Don't you dare set an alarm clock. This last week has been exhausting for you, I'm sure."

Kizzie looked over at the children playing in the corner, the boys building a wall around Zoe, Lulu swapping dolls with her to keep her distracted so she didn't 'help' them build it. "You're right. I'll just grab my blanket and…" She yawned, just the thought of a good night's sleep making her drowsy. "I don't think I'll say good-bye while they're having fun. I'll see you later. Or in the morning."

"In the *late* morning or afternoon," Bea corrected, and gave her a hug.

Kizzie grabbed the keyring with the lucky tee and Heath's house key, her snuggle blanket, and toothbrush then looked back. *How'd I get so blessed as to have friends like this?* She yawned again, then shut the door, ready for sleep. It didn't matter that it was four in the afternoon and the sun was still up. She'd never slept sixteen hours in a row but was ready to give it a try.

***

Rumble, rumble, clunk!

Kizzie sat up in bed and looked at the clock on the nightstand—two twenty. Was that 2:20 in the morning or afternoon? She pulled the black-out curtain aside and looked at the sky. It was daylight, but dim, either morning or a totally overcast afternoon. It was hard to tell in late June in Alaska.

Her heart raced as she tried to remember why she had been awakened so quickly. Right—it was the familiar mechanical groans of a garage door opener. But where was she? She never heard the garage door opening while at Bea's. Then a smile spread across her face. She was at

Heath's, sleeping in his bed, smelling his aroma on the pillow she had cuddled into as she fell asleep, fantasies swirling through her head of how wonderful life would be if he was hers, or better yet, her husband.

But who could be here now? Corporal Lent had dropped off Heath's car at the airport parking lot, but he wasn't supposed to be back for two more days. Her gut was tight—on high alert—as she listened to the kitchen door open and close. Slipping out of bed, she grabbed the bent golf club leaning against the wall in the corner and raised it to her shoulder, ready to assault an intruder. No one was going to steal from her man.

Ah, it's so good to be home. Just wait until I tell Bea that I not only found my aunt but my sister, too! I'd have been happy to find out where she lived just so I could visit her, but to find her as a full-grown woman, happy and with a career...

Fwap!

"Whoa, there!"

Heath reached up and grabbed the nine-iron before it thunked him in the head.

"Heath! What are you doing here?"

"I live here. And why are you here?" He looked at the

mussed-up sheets and smiled. "Not that I don't like the idea of you in my bed, but I sorta wanted to be here with you when that happened." He shook his head. "I mean…

"So, you want me in your bed?" she asked, then dropped her shared grip on the club and wrapped her arms around him.

"Oh, you have no idea," he said, then let the golf club fall to the ground and pulled her to him and kissed her like it was the only kiss they had left to share.

"Will you marry me?" he asked as Kizzie pulled away to take a breath.

"What? I mean, yes, but aren't we moving a little fast?"

His answer was to lift her up, allowing her the chance to wrap her legs around him as she had done less than two days ago.

"Mmm," he moaned, then loosened his grip on her bottom, allowing her to find her feet. "I think we should talk a little bit, but I'm fine with coming back to this in about," he looked at his watch, intending to call a two-minute time out for discussion, then saw the time. Phew! It was late, but he still had another day of leave before he had to go back to work.

"You're not going to give me a lecture on being too

forward or anything like that, are you?" she asked, biting her kiss-swollen lip in anticipation of admonishment.

"Oh, no, no. Every couple has their own time schedule. I'm happy to be on the fast track with you. No, I mean, yes, traditionally we're probably moving too fast, but frankly, I don't care what others think. When it's right, it's right. You're a good woman, Mackenzie soon-not-a-Wadsworth, and I intend to make you mine as soon as you tell me yes."

"But I just did, remember?" she said, then giggled.

"Just making sure that the 'aren't we moving too fast' didn't wipe out the yes part. Actually, I already found the venue, that is, if you're willing to relocate. I'm out of the service in just over a week. I won't have to get approvals and submit pounds of paperwork to marry you. All I'll need is your okay and a marriage license. Oh, and an officiate. This is one marriage I can't preside over."

Kizzie leaned in and kissed him below his earlobe, rubbing her nose on his neck, driving herself mad with his scent. "Do I get to know where?" she whispered.

"McMinnville, Or..." he said, the rest of the location cut off by her kiss.

"Ump!"

"Oops! Sorry," Kizzie said. "I thought you were finished. Okay, so we're going to be married in McMinnville, Oregon, right?" she asked, poised to attack him with kisses—and hopefully more—as soon as he said yes.

Heath put up one finger. "Hold on. I have to tell you more. If I don't, and you don't like what I have to share, then maybe you won't want to move to McMinnville. Or marry me…"

The thought of not having her in his life made his chest ache, his arms heavy. *What if she…*

"Heath King, look at me. Unless you have another wife stashed somewhere that you didn't tell me about, I will marry you. Zoe and I will relocate to wherever in the world—not just America—you say. Now, whatever your big secret is, you'd better tell me quick or I'll explode!"

"I did a DNA test and found a close match who turned out to be my mother's sister. The search started because I was looking for someone else, my little sister. You see, when I was five and she was one, my mother sent her away because she said she was broken. But she wasn't broken. She was just like Zoe. Special, but perfect."

Kizzie put her forehead on Heath's shoulder, letting him know how proud she was of his attitude but letting him continue his story uninterrupted.

"I contacted my aunt via email, she said she had something to tell me in person, I got the leave and flew and drove all night to see her and found out my aunt adopted Willa, my sister."

"Wow! That's a mouthful..." Kizzie disentangled herself from Heath then pulled on his hand to get him to sit next to her on the bed.

"So, do you still want to marry me?" he asked.

"You didn't tell me whether you already had a wife or not," she said, chewing back her grin.

"No, I've never had one. I've been waiting for you to show up. I have to tell you, though, there's more. My Aunt Nettie and her wife have a little business creating botanicals—lotions, soaps, teas—sort of like what you and Bea make. They want to take a twentieth anniversary road trip but can't leave Willa and the garden. I told them I'd be more than happy to help them out as soon as I'm out of the army."

Now Kizzie was excited in a different way. "Wait, you mean you not only discovered your former family and you want to take on Zoe and me as your new family, but you also have a career lined up? You won't have to look for a job?

And it's working with herbs and flowers and…" Kizzie wrapped her arms around him and squeezed his shoulders, holding back the compulsion to smother him with kisses in case he had more to share.

"There's also a little cottage on the property, a two-bedroom bungalow just perfect as a starter home for the new director of advertising and shipping coordinator."

"You told them you'd take it, didn't you?"

"I told them I'd have to ask my fiancée first," he said, "But not to let anyone else take it, just in case. Looks like life just keeps getting better and better."

"You got that right!" she said, ready to lunge.

"Before we…ahem…resume, why are you in my bed?"

"Oh, shoot! I'm sorry. I didn't expect you back and Bea said you wouldn't mind. I was going to wash the sheets tomorrow. Or I guess that would be today… Anyhow, I was going to return it to tip top shape after I got up. At Bea's, Zoe and I share the same twin bed. She moves around a lot, so I haven't been getting much sleep. Bea wanted me to get at least one good night's sleep so insisted I come over here. She's got Zoe covered. I'm not supposed to come back until tomorrow at lunch time. Or something like that. She just didn't want me to set an alarm or worry about taking care of Zoe or…"

Heath continued kissing her throat, doing his best to distract her. He knew what she meant.

"You know, it wouldn't be proper for the two of us to spend the night together, but it's been a long day and a half for me. It would also be extremely rude to Bea and Zeke for you to come traipsing in at three in the morning. I think we'll take a bogey on this one and have you spend the rest of the night here. There are some things I won't do until we're properly married," Heath said, then pulled her close, "but others are up for negotiation."

Kizzie came in close, as if to kiss him, paused, then said, "Let the negotiations begin," then moved in to finish what she had begun the day before. Experiencing true passion.

Chapter 12

Heath held Zoe in his arms, close but far enough away so she couldn't grab Willa's nose. "This is your niece, Zoe. Zoe, this is your Aunt Willa. She's my sister."

"Hello, Zoe. It's nice to meet you," Willa said, and reached up to try and shake Zoe's hand. "You get to live in the cottage over there, so I'll be able to see you every day. I'll take you in the garden with me if your mommy and daddy say it's okay." She turned to Heath. "So, you're a daddy *and* a bubba now, huh?"

"Yes, I am. And I'll always be. Even when I didn't know where you were, and you didn't remember me, I was always your bubba."

"I'm glad I don't have to decide who's the most beautiful one here. I think everyone is radiant," Bea said, as she looked around.

"Well, I'll make it easy, or maybe easier," Zeke said. "Without a doubt, Zoe is the cutest flower girl, Willa the prettiest maid of honor, my wife a truly awesome matron of honor, and of course, Kizzie is beyond belief as the bride."

"Yes, and the honorary mother-of-the-bride and mother-of-the-groom look pretty sharp, too," Bea added, then looked down at her crew. "And you're the best-looking attendants, children. Try to stay clean, at least until the photographer gets the pictures taken."

"When I get married," LuLu said, "I want to get married in Oregon, too. There are so many pretty flowers here!"

"Don't be in a rush to get married," Kizzie said, then knelt beside her. "Just wait until the right man…or woman…comes along. You'll know when it's right."

She stood up and turned to Bea, "Is everything all set for the beach houses? I mean, we'll only be half a mile up the beach if Zoe needs me or…"

"Or if you need me? Don't worry about us. You and Heath enjoy your honeymoon. I've been in Alaska for so long, I forgot that some beaches have sand and shells instead of rocks and mud! We'll have lots to keep us busy. I have plenty of hats, sunscreen, buckets and shovels, and a few kites. Oh, and Zeke bought a few boxes of those biodegradable golf balls that have a fish food core. He's going to smack a few of them into the ocean to see if he can improve his range. At least he won't have to worry about broken windows. Plus, without distance markers, only he will know how far out he hit them. This is one kind of fish story no one can dispute: the sea critters will eat the evidence."

"I can't believe it," Kizzie said. "Two months ago, I was a total mess. I had a rotten marriage, a philandering husband who wouldn't support his family or even acknowledge his daughter. I'm sorry for the way he died, but glad he's no longer miserable. Now, I have a wonderful husband and a sister-in-law, and I still have you and yours in my life, the most wonderful folks in the world who are as much family as friends."

"Yup," Bea said, squeezing Tommy then patting her belly, "No matter how hard you try to arrange life, surprise families can be the best."

** The End**

Other books by Dani Haviland

A Stingray Christmas: (First book in the Arlie Undercover series) Anchorage detective on medical leave travels from Alaska to Arizona to see for the first time the son he'd fathered as an anonymous sperm donor. Great and rotten surprises await the cop with the smartest smartphone around.

The Biggest Heart Ever: (Book two in the Arlie Undercover series) When would Arlie learn that trying to do everything by himself could be deadly—and make Charlene a widow before they were married?

Always a Bigger Fish: (Book three in the Arlie Undercover series) Back in Alaska, Arlie finds out he's a target. Will vacationing detective Billy Burke (from THE FAIRIES SAGA) have information to help nab the scalper?

THE FAIRIES SAGA SERIES (in order with novellas):

Naked in the Winter Wind: (lengthy novel) How does an older woman wind up as a young hottie in Revolutionary War era North Carolina? First book in the time travel series.

Ha'Penny Jenny: (historical novella) More about the naïve and psychic young girl who was adopted into a time traveling family. Will her past catch up to her?

Aye, I am a Fairy: (lengthy novel) Young British lord finds himself entwined with a time traveling family and must decide if he should go back in time, too. Second book in the series.

Dances Naked: (novel) Directionally challenged time traveler is rescued by Cherokee in 18ᵗʰ century. What must he do before the chief will show him to The Trees, the portal through time?

Chasing Christmas: (historical novella) A young Cherokee is rescued from an abusive man and changes the lives of many in this 18ᵗʰ century America family.

The Great Big Fairy: (lengthy novel) Very tall Benji grew up in the 20ᵗʰ century but was born in the 18ᵗʰ. When he finds a way to return to his grandparents in the distant past, he goes for it. Once there, he realizes he can't stay, but must return to the future. Fourth book in the series.

Little Bear and the Ladies: (historical novella) What's a bachelor trapper to do with all the females he rescues from the Hessian mercenaries? He'd better hurry and figure something!

Little Drummer Boy: (historical novella) Young Scout works to earn money for a home in post-Revolutionary War America but runs up against prejudices and snowstorms.

Never Too Young: (historical novella) Scout and Ha'Penny Jenny have grown up, but will they be able to spend their life together, or will the past and ruffians get in their way?

Time in a Little Blue Bottle (time travel 'mash up' novella) Elvis, Mark Twain, and the prime vampire are racing to get the bottle of Fountain of Youth water before sweet Bella and the youthful pickpocket. So why are time travelers Marty Melbourne and Master Simon interested?

CONTEMPORARY NOVELLAS – BENJI, THE LOST YEARS

Luke the Unexpected: Love of classic motorcycles brought them together, but Luke and Holly have other challenges to face. Find out how their friend Benji got his stripes here.

Pool Boy Wanted: No Experience Preferred (rather racy) Young Benji has been a hostage and slave, but life gets worse when an older woman decides she wants him as her own. (Also part of Unforgettable Suspense box set)

STAND ALONE NOVELLAS

Kit Kringle: An Alaskan Tale (contemporary) Kay moved to Alaska for the wrong reasons, then decided to stay and start her own business. What she hadn't planned on were prejudices and falling in love.

Be My Angel: Wyatt's dream to help save the wild mustangs began with the purchase of a rundown ranch in western Oregon. What he hadn't anticipated was being mesmerized by a sassy woman in a wheelchair.

Dani Haviland has never been one to believe, "You can't do that!" She started her own business in 1994, selling tractor parts in Alaska, then segued to writing and publishing books, becoming a *USA Today* bestselling author in the process. She currently splits her time between Alaska and Oregon, tirelessly writing and gardening, publishing and promoting, while claiming to be 'retired.'

Contact

Dani Haviland can be found at:

Website: www.danihaviland.com

Email: dani@dani.haviland@gmail.com

Facebook: Dani Haviland Author

and/or The Fairies Saga Fans

Twitter: @dani_haviland

BookBub: http://bit.ly/BBDani

Goodreads: http://bit.ly/2DHgdrds